Big League City

Big League City

Adam Breindel

Copyright © 2025 by Adam Breindel

No part of this publication may be reproduced, distributed, or transmitted in any form or by any means, including photocopying, recording, or other electronic or mechanical methods, without the prior written permission of the publisher, except as permitted by U.S. copyright law.

The story, all names, characters, and incidents portrayed in this production are fictitious. No identification with actual persons (living or deceased), places, buildings, and products is intended or should be inferred.

First Printing, 2025

To Zachary

"[E]very avalanche ... starts out the same way, when a single grain falls and makes the pile just slightly too steep at one point. What makes one avalanche much larger than another has nothing to do with its original cause, and nothing to do with some special situation in the pile just before it starts. Rather, it has to do with the perpetually unstable organization of the critical state, which makes it always possible for the next grain to trigger an avalanche of any size."

– *Mark Buchanan,* Ubiquity: Why Catastrophes Happen

1

"Too early in the morning to shoot somebody. Poor sap, he's half asleep still."

I froze in the near darkness. A tall silhouette in my kitchen held my own 9mm Beretta, the grip pinched disdainfully between thumb and forefinger like a fouled rag.

Reflex kicked in. I twisted to my right side in bed, stretched my arm to the nightstand shelf, and grabbed air. Something pulled deep in my shoulder and I grunted, both in pain and annoyance that my own gun now taunted me from across the room.

Looking up, I saw a mild grin spread across a barely visible face. The gun fell into a coat pocket.

"This thing is ancient and it's heavy as hell, Mr. Louis. You're not a young man anymore. You're likely to hurt yourself," said the shadow.

Another, shorter man emerged next to the first, twenty feet from me across the space that passed for my living room. The short man nodded silently and started poking through kitchen drawers.

I flopped onto my left side and swung my other arm against the wall, down behind the mattress. My hand ran all the way to the floor and came up empty.

Again, my guest was a step in front of me. "Now this," the tall began, holding what appeared to be the Springfield compact .45 I was futilely fumbling for behind my bed, "is still a bit heavy but at least you can nose it around."

He demonstrated and I faced the business end.

Out of aces, I rolled to my back and put both hands where he could see them. He handed the .45 to his associate, took three steps forward, swiveled my favorite chair, and sat down facing me.

"There's no need for any bluster or gunplay," he said, seemingly unaware of the irony. "We have a message to share. Nothing more."

"Haven't you heard of email? Or a telephone? You can't come breaking into a man's apartment and expect—"

He opened his coat revealing his own weapon, something large in a shoulder holster. "On the other hand, if you can't but fuss, well…"

I looked around. The apartment was dim in the early morning.

"Turn on a light or something, at least."

The short man removed a box of breakfast cereal from my cabinet and wandered over to flip on a small table lamp. He returned to the kitchen and asked, "Where do you keep the bowls?"

"What?" I asked. This was absurd. The tall one shushed me. They wore thin black coats and black beanies. They were white, fortyish, Portland pale, unremarkable.

The tall man whispered harshly to his associate, "Put that down and shut up."

I had calmed a bit but now felt a new rush of adrenaline. "What the hell is going on here?"

"Never mind him."

The short man found a bowl and a spoon.

"Listen to me!" the tall man exclaimed.

"OK, let's have it."

"First, you are Jack Louis, correct?"

"Who else would I be?"

"I'll take that as an affirmative. The message is this: You may be contacted soon by a woman, in connection with a job. The job may seem boring – a lot of real estate fine print and old land records. But she may offer you a lot of money. You don't want this job and you will not take it."

His statement was punctuated with a crunch from his associate, now deep in the bowl. A face popped up over the rim. "This stuff ain't bad."

I considered replying, wondering if distracting the cold breakfast connoisseur might give me an opening to get one of my guns back. My other guest gave a withering look.

"As I was saying, you can't take this job."

"What do you mean I can't take it? Are you threatening me?"

"Nothing like that. It's complicated and we don't have all of the details. But you can't, and it's best for you to know that ahead of time."

He stood up and waved his companion toward the door. "Put the bowl down." The bowl rapped against the kitchen counter followed by my two firearms, minus the magazines.

I jumped out of bed as they exited. Before I got across the room, the door slammed and they were gone.

Struggling to gather my wits, I stared at the nearly empty bowl of cereal neatly framed by two pistols. I grabbed the empty Springfield, hesitated momentarily – a nonfunctional gun could be more dangerous than no gun – went back to my desk for a full mag, swung the door open, and looked down the vacant hallway. I ran to the stairs and jumped down three at a time to the front vestibule. Opening the door, I looked up and down a barren street.

Stumbling back upstairs, I half expected to awaken, the entire encounter a dream. Spilled milk and cereal on the counter confirmed otherwise.

2

The rumpled bed looked appealing and I briefly considered going back to sleep. No chance. Might as well brew the coffee and clean up the mess.

Drawing the first few ounces of brew from the pot with an addict's desperation, I checked over my apartment. No indication of force – or even clumsy lock picking – on the door. Nothing but the spoon, bowl, and cereal were out of place. It wasn't obvious how they'd gotten behind my mattress without waking me. Could they have bugged the place, set cameras? I'd need to have it swept, which meant money I didn't have or calling in valuable favors. The decision would have to wait a bit.

Nothing about this made sense. I worked as a private investigator – most of the time – but the kind of case the men warned me about sounded like a boring job for a real estate attorney. While those gigs sometimes required investigation, and I'd be damned if some clowning thugs were going to put me off a job, the truth is that big landowners in Portland didn't need my flavor of snooping to get what they wanted.

An hour later, caffeine restlessness combined with unemployment had me pacing and ruminating, swiveling on a chair near the foot of the bed. Some months back, the local political toddler contingent had blown up my office. Landlord collected an insurance check and wasn't sure he even wanted to rebuild. In moments like these, I missed having the routine of a walk to the office, a destination and focal point. I'd take a walk somewhere else, I thought, picking up scraps of Amazon boxes and a piece of styrofoam from the floor. My place was basic and outdated. But it was clean and it wasn't shabby. OK, it was more than a little shabby.

As I considered destinations, a soft, brown – nearly black – head poked from under the bed.

"It's OK, the strange visitors are gone. That must have been pretty scary. Honestly I was a little scared myself."

I crouched as a feline body emerged and nuzzled against my knee, then my wrist.

"OK, Cocoa, let's get you some food."

She wasn't even supposed to be my cat, but that's a long story. I set up her food and water, grabbed my coat, phone, and gun, took a long careful last look around the apartment, and headed out.

I was wandering west on Couch Street in the hazy October morning, weaving around gently drifting clumps of garbage, stepping over piles of syringes. Tarps flapped in entrance ways. The folks who'd left this detritus were getting breakfast on Burnside or nearby. Hopefully. Too often, addicts who weren't still here sleeping in the morning had been driven off to a hospital – or the morgue – overnight.

Just a few blocks later, shiny condos sprouted where uniformed men and women pressure sprayed the evening's evidence off the cement.

My phone buzzed. And again. It was a Spanish woman's name I didn't recognize at first but she was in my contacts so I must have met her. The contact didn't bear the telltale symbol I appended to represent "hostiles," so, what the hell? I picked up.

"Oh hello, Mr. Louis? This is Mr. Louis?" The vowels were particularly rich but the English was clear.

"Hello, Mrs. Nuñez. This is Jack Louis."

"You do not probably remember me. But maybe you remember my boy on the baseball team, the pitcher, Fernando?"

It came back right away – Fernando Nuñez was a solid slot in the rotation for the Yamhill-Newberg Pioneers, a minor league ball club just over half an hour and, culturally, half a world away from Portland. At their ballpark, I had shared the front row behind the home dugout with his mother, Altagracia Nuñez, for three games over two days the previous summer. She had been in Oregon from the Dominican Republic to visit her son. We watched him throw an impressive five-hit performance as well as pound a game-winning double in blazing August heat.

I was slightly acquainted with Fernando's host family near Yamhill and – since both the town and the ball club are small operations – I'd been invited to an informal dinner with Fernando, his mom, the host family, and a bunch of other folks from the club, including George Delany, the largest individual owner of the team.

"Of course I remember you, Mrs. Nuñez. Is everything OK? What is Fernando up to in the off season?"

"Mr. Louis, I don't know who else I can call. I think Fernando is in trouble. Not in the ... in the village. In the city. You help people in trouble in the city, right? For your job?"

"Well I try to, but tell me: what makes you think Fernando has a problem in Portland?"

"He left me a voicemail. He was doing a job for the owners, bringing important papers to Portland. He was driving a car for them and he got into a crash."

"Is he OK? I am happy to help him get the car to a repair shop. Do you have his number? I can text him…"

"I don't know. I don't know if he's OK. He didn't get hurt in the crash, it was – what do you call it? A fender bender? But that's not the problem. The real problem. Some men attacked him. They beat him and took the papers. He ran away. He said he is hiding. In the city. Where you are. I wrote it down. Here it is. In his message he said he was across from a hotel called Multnomah. Then I have not been able to call him. Or text him. Do you know this hotel?"

"The Multnomah? Yes, I do. I have worked there a little and I have a friend there. We can look for Fernando there right away."

"Oh, thank you. Thank you, Mr. Louis. I am so worried."

3

Now I had a place to go and a reason to do it. With a 180-degree turn, I began walking toward The Multnomah.

Downtown hotels often needed ad hoc security assistance, preferably compensated in kind and performed by someone neither an employee nor a contractor. I helped out in the role at a number of places, so I knew all the staff. And, anyway, it was never a bad day to work The Multnomah.

Although its surroundings were particularly grubby this morning, the glorious cut stone edifice could still catch the breath in your throat when you rounded the corner and the structure slid into view. A sibling property to Henry Villard's Portland Hotel – long since demolished and now the source of ghosts haunting Pioneer Square – The Multnomah was a survivor and a century-old contrast to successive waves of architectural style.

As each design fashion had dawned, a new building would briefly make The Multnomah look outdated, then technically obsolete, later inhospitable, irrelevant … and after a bit, somehow, the new style would become less compelling. Regional and world troubles somehow became associated with ideas embedded in the new architecture, and then The Multnomah would feel oddly enticing, nostalgic, then impressive, rising and blooming in the local imagination. It would admonish and, in the end, gently tolerate the wayward successive generations.

As my friend and associate Manny Gil, the property's head of security operations, reminded me from time to time with a grin: "There's a reason she's still here, ya know." Manny was a New England transplant who had come into security through the side door. In sum, the world had decided he was a better security ops guy than bouncer after deciding he was a better bouncer than musician. I had seen him in all those roles and more and he was always solid. I liked what remained of his old band, Manny and the Gillfish, too. Then again, maybe there was a reason I never had a gig with *The Rocket* or *Rolling Stone*.

As far as finding Fernando, unless I bumped into him on the street outside, Manny with his army of all-seeing digital sensors was the best place to start. I circled the building, then checked the eight surrounding blocks to no avail before heading inside.

Manny handed me a cup of "wicked strong" (his words) coffee in his claustrophobic linoleum-tile-fluorescent-bulb office and I shared what Altagracia Nuñez had told me. I supplemented it with a bit of background on Fernando, the ball club, and the financial and social pressures that might lead a man to moonlight as courier for the team's rich backers.

"So you didn't see anything at all in the area outside?" he asked.

"Nothing. But if he was really on your block here, I was hoping the camera system would at least tell us which direction he went."

"We can definitely do that. We have a new assistant who... Wait a second. You're gonna love this. Do you have a picture of the man?"

"Not personally, but we can find one online. Worst case, I can ask his mother to send me one."

"Excellent. So we can take that photo and run an automated search through all of our recent camera footage. The AI will do the heavy lifting in just a few minutes."

I whistled for effect. Poorly. "That's a handy trick. But I thought Portland banned facial recognition a few years back?"

"Well, let's just say out-of-touch politicians trying to regulate cutting-edge tech is rarely a success. And the commissioners who passed the ban understood as much about computers as your cat does about quantum physics." Manny giggled a bit at his own joke.

"So you're saying there's a loophole or something that could make my life easier?"

"Man, it's all loopholes." He tossed his empty coffee cup against the wall, attempting a bank shot into the trash. He missed and a few drops of coffee splattered the floor where the cup landed. "Goddammit." He wiped the floor and threw away the cup. "It's my own office. I gotta clean this or live with the filth. But hey! While the AI is doing its thing, let's take a quick walk around."

We planned to walk the lobby and the conference rooms but began at the front desk with a pic on Manny's phone.

"Any chance you saw this guy around earlier this morning?"

Manny looked at me. "Morning, right?" I nodded.

The tall, tattooed desk clerk, Axel per his badge, rubbed his chin and said, "Nah, definitely not."

"Wait!" a voice called out to Manny and me.

A chubby thirties pink-and-blonde dye job in a blazer and leggings called out as she glided from some back office to the desk. "Axel didn't start until an hour ago. I was covering the desk and I checked this man in." She started typing on a computer terminal.

"You checked him in? He's here?"

"Yes. I mean, I guess he's here. I definitely checked him in. Axel and I had eyes on the lobby since then and we didn't see him leave." She turned the monitor partly around and pointed. "Here's his room. One night, prepaid. We just took a hold for incidentals."

Manny and I thanked the manager and vigorously headed to the elevator. We got off on the fourth floor and I followed Manny down the hall to 410.

He knocked using his keyring in the hotel manner, generating extra noise, sparing the knuckles. No response.

He knocked again. Again no response.

He turned to me. "You want to try?"

"Sure," I said. "Mr. Nuñez! Mr. Nuñez, it's Jack Louis! You don't remember me but I talked with your mother!"

Silence.

"Mr. Nuñez, your mother said you told her you were in a car crash and had a problem last night. She is worried about you. She called me from the D.R. this morning."

Nothing. I turned to Manny. "Let's go in."

He pulled his key. "This is kind of on the edge here, Jack. You're not working for him and there's no evidence of a crime here."

"Think of it like a wellness check. His mom called me from the Dominican Republic for chrissake after only meeting me twice in her life. That has to count for something."

"Technically, not a lot, but you've taken enough risks for me. Fuck it."

He opened the door.

The room was in disarray. Bedclothes on the floor, lamp broken next to a line of what might have been blood.

"Here's your evidence of a crime."

Manny's face was grim as we stepped into the room. We both expected to find Fernando unconscious, probably injured, and, we hoped, nothing worse.

Five minutes later we were relieved we did not find a body but troubled that the room held no obvious trace of Fernando.

I knew the cops wouldn't be able to help yet, or maybe ever, looking for an adult who wasn't where his mother expected him to be. "Could we at least get some attention with 'Defrauding an Innkeeper' or something like that?" I asked Manny.

He shook his head. "The stay was paid for. He departed on time. The incidentals hold will more than cover the broken lamp. And he's an athlete? They are more likely than average to pull a rockstar: toss the place and bail. Cops won't care; even the hotel doesn't care. Except me of course."

I had one last idea. "Do me a favor? Lemme spend a little extra time going over the room?"

"Not a problem." Manny shrugged and exited, letting the door swing closed behind him.

4

I poked around in the obvious places – under the mattress, behind the ironing board. There aren't too many places to hide stuff in a basic hotel room. I checked two favorites: ventilation ducts and toilet tank.

Closing the toilet lid and sitting for a moment to think, one more spot came to mind. Hotel vanity sinks typically have faux doors or drawers on the front which detach so the plant guys can get to the P-trap when guests gum up the works or drop an engagement ring. I reached under the panel to find a metal latch on a spring – a bit like trying to open the engine hood on an unfamiliar car but with smaller odds of a second-degree burn. When the latch popped, I swung a big panel onto the floor.

Inside, resting on a ledge, was an old-school interoffice mail envelope, the kind with the reusable grid of deliver-to lines and a winding string closure. Manila envelopes like this are not unheard of inside appliances, plumbing, or electrical boxes: documentation for the next unfortunate needing to decipher and repair the installation. But I grabbed it to take a look anyway.

There were no markings on the outside. I unwrapped the string and pulled out a sheaf of around twenty pages They were titled "Portland Stadium Rezoning Contingency." I had no idea what that was. About five of the pages were land plats with tons of minuscule markings.

The remainder was equally inscrutable legalese. The header and footer of each page read, "All-Star Summer LLP." I snapped the sink panel back into place and headed for the door, carrying the envelope.

Turning the door knob, I thought about who might be able to help me decipher the docs. A split second later, I realized I should have been attending to the peephole before opening up.

The door swung violently inward, smashing into my face and knocking me backward to the floor. A man in coveralls, a painter's cap, and a Covid-style surgical mask barreled through the opening. His eyes moved to the envelope in my hand and I reflexively pulled it close to my body as I scrambled backward along the floor to put a few feet between this man and myself.

I leapt up as he strode towards me and I moved on a diagonal to catch only a fraction of knuckle to the jaw. I dug for his solar plexus with my right fist, but he was moving too fast so I missed, catching rib instead.

So far, I was on the losing end of this encounter. The hotel was – more or less – my turf and I only needed to escape with the envelope, so I grabbed the man in an improvised clinch, the envelope still in my left hand, and spun him around so my back was to the door. I rotated out of the clinch, putting my right elbow into his underarm and tried to sweep his leg.

I managed to break free, gained almost six feet of distance, and started pulling the door open. But the damper was stiff and the sound-suppressing door heavy. Just as it opened enough for me to get out, I felt a tickle brush my side and then the bracing shock of what must have been ten thousand volts.

My body convulsed backward and I fell to the floor. Simultaneously, my head exploded in pain along with a bright flash and wave of nausea. Vision blurred. I didn't lose consciousness entirely, but, fifteen seconds later, when I could move again, the room was empty and the envelope was gone. I got to my feet, checked the fisheye peephole this time, and exited into an empty hallway. A few minutes later I made it to Manny's office.

"You look a little ... shaken up," he said as soon as he saw me.

"A few thousand volts' worth. I found some docs – they must have been the ones Fernando was carrying that got him attacked. But I had a little encounter trying to get out of the room and I lost them."

I lifted my shirt. Two red welts stood out where the stun gun had blasted me. "Voltage bounced me on my ass."

"A microcoulomb at least," Manny said.

"Huh?"

"It's not the voltage, it's microcoulombs. Electric charge. Never mind, you'll appreciate the detail later. Anyway, take a look: this is your guy, right?"

He clicked something and we watched video of Fernando on three channels. On the left-hand screen, an elevator camera captured the tall pitcher sandwiched between two men in dark coats and hats. I wondered whether there was any possibility these were the guys who visited me for breakfast.

On the center screen, a lobby camera caught them exiting the elevator, the two men brusquely steering Fernando around a corner and into a broad, gallery-like passage.

The Multnomah occupied a full city block and, on two sides, there were ground-floor businesses facing the street. Some of those were accessible from both the street and from corridors inside the hotel off the lobby: a fancy wine bar, a haberdasher-cum-outfitter playing up the "northwest expedition" theme, and PDX Homestyle Cafe. The last was an upscale, regional take on down-home classics and its owner had built it into a Portland institution, beloved as much by locals as by the hotel guests.

On Manny's far right display, the two men prodded Fernando down the hallway and through the door into the Homestyle Cafe. We couldn't see anything further. Presumably they'd exited the cafe directly to the street. Nevertheless, I decided to follow their route out.

"I'll head out that way and chat with Amelia," I told Manny, referencing the cafe's owner. "Then I'll try to figure out what to tell poor Altagracia Nuñez. She's worried to death, three thousand miles away, and I don't even know if Fernando is still in one piece. Not a conversation I'm looking forward to." Manny clasped me on the shoulder and gave me a sympathetic look.

Still shaken from getting jumped like a fool, my head swiveled as I exited the security office and traversed the hotel's ground floor in the footsteps of the men on the surveillance video. From the elevator, I headed to the restaurant.

The door was unlocked but most of the lights were off and the place was dead quiet.

I called out: "Hey! Anyone here?"

The cafe should have been open, if not bustling. And it wasn't wise to leave the till unattended, even for a bathroom break, in this part of town. Someone was liable to walk in and take the entire register, and, in fact, exactly that had occurred a few times this year.

The shuffle of feet drew my attention and I turned to see Amelia Schultz emerge from the office next to the kitchen. Amelia was a fiftyish graying blonde and a touch overweight but usually appeared with flawless makeup, stylish clothing, jewelry, something attractive adorning her hair: appearance was critical when it was "upscale" branding that turned crab cakes or a pot pie into a twenty-five-dollar entree.

I hadn't been in to eat or to visit in a couple of weeks but right away something was wrong. Amelia looked as if she hadn't slept, washed, or run a brush through her hair. She wore a gray oversized T-shirt and black leggings. For the first time I could recall, she looked her age or worse.

"Hi Jack," she greeted me.

Something was off. My question – whether she or her staff had seen the guys exit with Fernando and could supply any additional info – could wait.

"Is everything OK? Isn't the house usually open this time of day?"

"Yeah. I've been meaning to invite you, Jack. We're going to do a little drink thing one of these nights, kind of say thanks to everyone and have a good cry."

She looked on the verge of tears herself.

"I must be missing something."

"The folks in the hotel didn't say anything? We're shutting down. Twenty-two fucking years and we're shutting down." Anger bubbled and pushed the tears back. "Here," she said, walking around behind the bar. Reaching underneath, she pulled out two coffee mugs. "Have a mug. Have two of them."

These weren't six-dollar logo mugs. The cafe served hot drinks out of artisan stoneware in attractive, glazed earth-tone patterns. The name of the restaurant was embossed on a sort of raised tablet. She ran her left thumb over the word "Homestyle" on one of them, pushed them both at me across the bar, dabbed at a tear with her right hand, and then angrily muttered, "Fuckers."

"What happened?"

"Eight times this year, assholes have broken in. I don't know why. There's no cash here. Nothing valuable. They take the register and sometimes some booze. Eight times we cleaned it up, replaced the glass." She took a deep breath and emitted a sigh. "It's not cheap fitting a big single pane into the historic facade here. But we did it. We weren't going to give in. *I* wasn't going to give in or give up on this town. We were on the news. We're in every guidebook, you know. People used to come from California to eat *here*."

Proud, and defiant, she gestured at the bar and the tables beyond.

"A week ago they did it again but this time they lit a fire in the kitchen. Homeless? Druggies? Lunatics? All three? We have a good security system. Fire and rescue got here quick. But a ton of equipment got destroyed, along with parts of the ceiling, electrical, and, ironically, fire suppression. Insurance might cover the hardware, but the timeline for permitting and review, designs to current standards and working in this beautiful old building... It would take years. We could move, maybe get going again in a year. But I just can't do it. You remember we moved once. It was never the same and I just don't have it in me to do it again."

My gut folded and twisted. I heard variations of this story a couple of times a month. Still, for each owner, calling it quits was a death in the family. For the city, whose modern identity was linked to quirky independent businesses, where the famous food scene was one of the only value-add industries, it was a fathom's drop farther into unknown depths.

"I'm sorry," was all I could come up with.

"Well. Yeah. I still can't really believe it. But I'm working on the accounting here today, closing out all the books. My people and suppliers need to get paid and they will." Amelia's thoughts seemed to drift off for a moment but then snapped back: "You were coming in just to say hi? Or grab a coffee? I do have coffee!"

"Actually, I am working on a sort of a case. Earlier today, three men came in here from the hotel –"

"Oh, yeah. I saw that. I hadn't locked the inside door but the lights were off. They came in: two white guys in coats and a tall Latino guy, almost like they were horsing around or something. The white guys kept jostling the other one, even though he was bigger than them. Before I could even tell them we weren't open, they wrestled their way across the dining room and went out the front door. Was locked but it's got a crash bar – you can always push it open from the inside."

"You said they 'wrestled' their way?"

"Yeah they were messing around, pushing each other, pushing the tall guy anyway. He didn't really push back. Flipped a chair or two but not a big deal, especially given the circumstances."

She walked to where one of the chairs was knocked over and picked it up. I traced the path from there to the door. Under a nearby table was a small paper ball. I uncrumpled it. A header read "Portland Stadium Rezoning Contingency" and it bore page number 59. The sheet was missing the bottom third but it didn't much matter as the paper appeared blank beneath the header. I folded it and put it in my pocket.

"I'm really sorry about everything, Amelia. PDX Homestyle Cafe will be missed. It's gonna leave another hole in the heart of this city. But I'd love a chance to have one more drink with you and your crew. I can get the details from Manny?"

"Sure. Good luck with the case, Jack," Amelia said as she turned and headed back to the tiny office next to the kitchen.

I stepped out into the mild mid-autumn breeze. Darker clouds marbled white ones in a turbulent sky. It felt nice. But we had turned the hard corner and summer wouldn't be back.

5

Heading west toward my apartment building, I hopscotched piles of human excrement speckling the sidewalks. I improved my dexterity and contributed to the cause of justice: two deeply self-important members of the city council insisted that cleaning sidewalks would be culturally insensitive and represent inequitable treatment. After all, there were (theoretically) people inheriting a meaningful tradition of dysentery. In any case, the councilors' neighborhoods lacked excrement – randomly, I'm sure, or due to natural diversity in the distribution of dysentery enjoyers.

When I got back to my building, I took a careful look all the way around the perimeter. Before heading upstairs, I entered El Dorado, a semi-famous gay bar and strip club operating on the ground level. Inside was cool, dark, and entirely empty save for the owner, Logan, carrying a case of booze around the end of the bar.

"Jack! You picked a dull time if you've decided to weigh new options and check out the show," Logan called out with a wink, gesturing toward two dark stages where performers danced several nights a week. Logan felt, I think, obligated to make a joke every time the unglamorous straight guy in the nondescript PI duds stumbled through.

"Afraid I'm still playing for the other team, but I do love feeling welcome," I shot back. "You just opened up?"

"Yep, about twenty minutes ago. Loaded in a bunch of booze, new glasses, and some T-shirts." He gestured toward a pile of fabric.

"See anyone or anything unusual when you were parking or loading?"

"Nope, nobody. Why? Sleuthing close to home?"

"Something like that. A couple of weirdos paid me a visit earlier this morning and I just got Tased on the job – well, stun-gunned – for the first time in three years. Not sure if the two incidents are related."

"Got it. Well, things seem chill now. Hopefully they stay that way. You better get upstairs, though: I could hear your cat mewling through the window over the street. I think she's hungry."

"I think she's hungry for attention," I said, half grinning. I waved and went outside, upstairs, and into my place. I locked the door, sat down, called the cat over, and began to think.

I spread out the page from the floor of the restaurant, opened my laptop, and punched "Portland Stadium Rezoning Contingency" into a bunch of searches, commercial databases, and AIs. The AIs had charming recommendations for unrelated topics but, otherwise, I got nothing. I emailed the office of Jeffrey Spencer, a plugged-in attorney with whom I'd collaborated on several cases in the past. More precisely, I wrote an email to his assistant and paralegal, Amy Shaw. She was as smart and as snarky as Jeffrey, but also knew how to playact an ironic rendition of a 1960s secretary as part of the big man's big-man act. She could also gather intel from a deep set of off-the-record sources.

If Amy had some down time, she might be able to dig up more in databases I couldn't afford or among contacts I couldn't stand. More likely, those contacts couldn't stand me or couldn't tolerate being seen with me. My ego insisted I return the favor.

Then I pulled the chair to the window and stared out at the sky, trying to assemble everything I knew about Fernando Nuñez, his mom, and the ball club. I opened the window so the cool air could keep me alert. Light filtered through chasms in the towering cumulus blowing northward. I was reciting dry facts to myself about Nuñez. They were unhelpful facts I already knew.

After two or three minutes, I felt a surprising, mild gust. I looked upward and caught a gap right through the clouds to a patch of deep blue. I stared straight into that blue spot and in an instant I was elsewhere.

6

It was a blistering ninety-degree day in August and I sat in Municipal Stadium. The sun cooked the blue polyethylene seats and the back of a seat, in turn, roasted my skin painfully through my T-shirt. The whitewashed concrete of the dugout hurt to look at despite my dark sunglasses. A spotless dome of near-violet – that color out the window of an airliner when you look straight up – arched over a field of British racing green so deep and smooth that I dismissed it as fake until I saw a divot tear off, attached to one of the players' cleats.

That player was Fernando Nuñez and I learned his name not from the announcer, the game program, or the scoreboard, but from the woman sitting next to me, who was cheering in Spanish and whom I had mistaken to be one of the town's many Latin residents. The stadium was small, our seats by the low wall beyond which infield skin ran fifteen feet or so to the first base line.

The tall man in the Pioneers gold and white uniform ran straight at us off the pitcher's mound and leaned across the barricade to hug the woman. He wore a gold chain with a tiny enamel flag in the red, white, and blue of the Dominican Republic mounted on a medallion in the shape of the island nation. I have to admit I didn't recognize the shape, so I appreciated the flag tipoff. He called her *"mami"* and she called out *"Fernandito!"* She glowed, in tears, as he leaned over the infield wall to embrace her. I smiled and Fernando held out his hand. I shook it as he breathlessly explained: "My mom – it's her first time seeing me play pro ball! Only her second time *en Los Yunais* – she's never been west of New York!"

I looked at her and said, "If your boy keeps throwing like he's doing today, he'll be in the major leagues." Which was true: Fernando had started the game and struck out eight batters in four innings and only given up one hit. As the teams swapped places to start the fifth, the stadium filled with the sound of a country-pop crossover starlet. They had been playing her hits all afternoon – a sort of theme day, it seemed – and I wondered how a tiny team like this class-A club afforded the rights.

Maybe I was too cynical. See, Yamhill County is a crossroads: barely a dozen miles over the hills from Portland, but filled with small towns tucked into farms and woodland. Another half hour's drive in Oregon's compact and undeveloped geography took you to the edge of settlement and beyond: dirt tracks – or no tracks – lost among wild mountains, violent rivers, and vacant canyonlands.

Here, between Yamhill and Newberg, and right about midway between the small skyscrapers and the giant elk, bulky guys in camo shorts with military tattoos and dirt-creased hands sat next to glossy blonde girls and took in the game alongside heavy lesbian couples in undercuts and muscle shirts. During inning switch, as the song's chorus poured from the PA, a few of the guys kept sipping their beers but the rest of the men and damned near every female in the place – save Altagracia Nuñez – were stomping and singing along.

Oregon was nothing if not extremes. Latter-day pioneers fought a hardscrabble living out of nothing but the ground, stiffly proud in the struggle. Portland's urban center attracted utopian collectivists aiming at a hope-filled but violently incompatible vision of frontier. Factions were entrenched, armed clashes an accepted part of the landscape. Casualties were expected and routine since the state had avoided building the suburban "political crumple zones" – in the form of a hundred thousand bored normies – that kept urban and rural extremists off each other's necks in other places.

If a minor league ball club and some urban cowboy musical stylings could yield an armistice in a cultural civil war, then perhaps we'd do well with another league and a troupe of angsty blondes in sequins and boots delivering refurbished if eternally mythical latter-day Americana.

The music stopped as the men on the field got to work, Pioneers eventually sweating it out to a five-one victory, visiting Eels scoring their lone run in the eighth against the closer after Fernando wrapped seven shutout innings.

At the end of the game, Fernando asked his mother to meet him outside the gate. He was going to shower and take her next door to eat. I walked out alongside Altagracia. She asked, "You will come, eat with us?"

I felt a bit awkward, imagining myself odd company at a family dinner. I started to make a polite excuse and say goodbye. A booming voice interrupted me. "Nonsense, Jack! The whole team, family, friends – we're going next door. You too!"

My confusion must have shown on my face. The owner of the voice was a graying man about seventy in a U of O polo, chinos, and loafers. He was a full head bigger than me, sweating lightly and carrying a blazer over his arm. "George Delany. You have a good time today?" He smiled. "You better have had a good time." I was even more confused.

"It's my ball club, son. Well, not a hundred percent mine. But that don't matter. Hell of a game today. Great crowd. Oh. And, yeah, I know who you are."

That was almost worrisome. I'd never worked a case here. Why I was even in Yamhill that day is a story for another time. But I liked to stay in the shadows where practical, even back home in Portland.

"You know Lenny and Peggy Owens, yeah?" he continued. "Peggy is my cousin. I know everybody in town. Even the ones who spend their time in the big city and only show up once in a blue moon. Peggy and Lenny, they're setting up to be a host family soon – at the end of the season. Maybe Fernando's host family."

I wasn't sure what to say, so I merely extended my hand and said, "It's great to meet you. Love the team."

He went right on: "So we're all going to the saloon and that means you too." He gestured along the sidewalk, which paralleled the right field line, to the structure immediately past the stadium. The saloon was a historic building, part brick and part wood. The stadium went directly up to it, nearly touching, so that the saloon's west wall formed part of the right field fence.

The story was that the stadium almost didn't get built there – some dispute over a strip of land belonging to the saloon's original owner confronted a league rule insisting on dimensions for the outfield. Apparently a compromise was reached and a close look revealed fine metal mesh that protected 19th century siding from home runs and long foul balls.

At that point, Fernando emerged from the locker room, hugged his mom again, and shook hands with George, who clapped him heartily on the back. We strolled the eighty yards or so in the slackening afternoon sun and entered the cavernous saloon. It seemed as if the entire town was already there with more coming in: players, friends, host families, random folks all looking for beer, chicken wings, tacos, hot dogs, and more beer.

A couple of young men looked like they just got off work at the wine country bed-and-breakfasts; three women came in still wearing Fred Meyer work shirts. On another wall was a pair of cops and some young men in coveralls from a Newberg quick lube outfit and engine repair. Wandering past, I caught snippets of a conversation about their own experiences playing high school ball. Baseball was big in Oregon and one of the cops had played at OSU with a couple guys who'd been drafted. About a third of the crowd were Latino workers, businessmen, and their families. A wealthy-looking couple in winery polos gnawed chicken tenders. It wasn't Portland diversity, I chuckled to myself, but just maybe a touch of the real thing.

There was music – loud music – and chatting was difficult. But spirits were buoyant and I consumed a solid portion of hot tacos and cold lager before people started drifting out. I joined them, since I had a stop to make in town before returning to Portland.

7

Suddenly I was back in my apartment, reverie interrupted when Cocoa leapt up and landed in my lap. I took a deep breath and called Mrs. Nuñez back, sharing most of what had happened but omitting the blood in Fernando's hotel room. That detail wasn't going to help a distant parent.

When I got off the call, my phone showed a message from Amy. Lawyers and old people are the only ones who still talk on the telephone, so I stood up and called her. I winced at a twinge in my knee – I might be joining one of those groups myself and I'd never taken the bar.

"Any luck?" I asked.

"No." Amy was direct. "If this 'Stadium Rezoning Contingency' is a thing, it's been kept tightly under wraps. Not totally surprising. Jeffrey and I get pulled into fighting these things for clients: the city and state talk big about openness and transparency, but keep as much secret as they can and go to court to keep it that way. Of course, we usually beat them." She giggled sarcastically. "But as for this stuff, no hint it exists."

"So we've got nothing?"

"Oh yes. I mean, no. I mean, I've got something better for you. We've got a mole inside Portland Permitting and Development and she's willing to give you a private orientation to the matter. You just need to wait until the end of the workday and be discreet. Apparently, there's quite a bit to this stadium plan and the goal is for some parts to avoid scrutiny."

"You have a mole? Like, a spy?"

"Something like that. Essential to the business."

"You run your own spies? You don't call me? I'm hurt!" I joked.

We both knew I could get away with a lot of things, but passing among politicos and their in-the-know bureaucrats wasn't one of them. The damned cocktail parties were the one place in Portland I couldn't blend in. I tried to bring game with the expensive suit, shoes, hair products, an exfoliating scrub, neutral high-register English ... but something about my posture or mannerisms always gave me away. Too many ambushes in my life left me in a perpetual starting-line crouch. Metaphorically. And physically and emotionally, if I'm honest. My unconscious sells me out.

Then, when I'm made, I still can't share, so people decide I'm a gangster. After all, who else struggles to hide years of street fighting under $9000 of designer wool and fails comically right out the gate?

If I play high-end security instead, people will buy it. My debonair competitors can have the cocktail circuit; I need to play to my strengths since the alternative is downright embarrassing. Anyway, that meant I was grateful for Jeffrey's and Amy's spy network.

"Is this connected to that Portland Field Project?" I asked. "The ones who have been trying to bring a major league team to the city? Like how the hell do you keep anything about a giant stadium development secret?"

"Go ask Jimmy Hoffa."

"Touché."

"OK, I'll let Hannah take it from here. Hannah Bowman. Tiny brunette. She'll be wearing a beret and a navy jacket. Meet her under the west end of the Marquam Bridge at 6:20 p.m."

"Marquam – that's the freeway bridge, right?"

"That's the one."

I thanked Amy and disconnected.

Portlanders mostly know their bridges but no one calls that one the Marquam Bridge. What was down there exactly? It was past the River Place development but before the hospital.

A light bulb went on: there was an odd little park underneath, where South River Parkway ends. It was pretty but required enduring the ear splitting racket of at least eight lanes of traffic overhead. On the other hand, no one could eavesdrop.

8

A little after five, I grabbed a jacket, a baseball cap, and a subcompact 9mm SIG and headed for the Orange Line.

After being on the receiving end of too many bullets earlier in the year, I'd decided to upgrade my firepower from the .380 – at least in cool weather, when clothing afforded concealment for the slightly bigger gun. Leaning against the brick facade of a bar waiting for the MAX, I reflected on a recent incident where a man with both a hatchet and machete had taken the joint hostage in the middle of the afternoon and threatened to kill the patrons. Although cops saved the day that time, Portland's meager force typically took half an hour to respond to priority calls, making firearms a necessity.

With a loud ring, the train pulled up.

I rode to South Waterfront, then walked to the meeting spot along South Bond at the river. My forehead and nose wrinkled. I was pretty sure this street didn't even exist last time I was down here; now there was a shiny road and a bike path. Still, aside from the hospital and the tram base, it was empty lots, parking spaces, and gravel fields wrapped in chain link.

Leaning against the railing as the sun slid behind the West Hills, I observed flocks of geese flying south, low over the river, and larger flocks of crows, higher up, headed north into town for the evening. The freeway bridge obscured Hood, but clouds swirling around the mountain were an explosion of neon pink against an indigo sky.

My phone buzzed with a text from Mrs. Nuñez. "The family where Fernando lives. They can help. They know he does extra work for the team. They give him a car to use. Talk to them. Please. Thank you."

If I couldn't locate Fernando soon, contacting the host family was a solid idea. I texted back: "I will talk to them. Thank you."

"Jack?"

A female voice emerged over the roar of traffic and I looked up. A truly petite woman in a blue coat, sharp beret, short skirt and black leggings walked toward me. Technically, Amy's description fit, but Hannah wasn't what I expected. She had *haute-couture*-runway looks and only her height – five feet if that much – could have kept her out of the modeling world. Her looks would turn heads even in jaded SoCal and she must've drawn a crowd in the far less sexy PNW.

Portland often seemed populated by kids no one would talk to in junior high and who, in a questionable effort to "reclaim the marginalization," adopted the look of comically overweight *Firefly* reavers. Next to that, Hannah looked like she belonged to a different species altogether. I bet she glitched locals' brains so bad they didn't see her at all.

My mind finally registered that she'd been speaking to me for a good two minutes. My mouth was wide open. With effort, I closed it.

No point starting off with bullshit, I figured, so I apologized, admitted I may be lacking some manners, stuttered my name, shook her hand, and sheepishly asked if she could start over again.

9

With a breezy Gen Z declaration of "not a problem, Jack," she pointed along the riverfront and began:

"The part everyone knows – at least everybody interested – is that Portland may get a Major League Baseball team and may build a stadium for that team roughly in that spot over there. MLB is a prestige brand and demands many things beyond just a place to sell seats and hot dogs. So these blocks here," she continued, with more gestures and pointing, "will be a mixed use district. An actual neighborhood, high end. Have you seen the area around Petco Park in San Diego? A bit smaller but that kind of a setup. Here's a picture."

I expected a rendering – architectural sketch or some AI-powered visualization – but what she showed me on her phone was a gray-and-white plat with text too small to resolve. All I could see were a few streets and the river.

"OK," I said. "I might need to take a closer look at that if the details matter."

"I can send you a copy of this version: it's the official version. But none of what matters is on this map. Here's the interesting part." She slowly looked around. We were alone. Despite the traffic, her voice dropped close to a whisper. "No one will build anything here. They can't. The land is basically worth less than zero, and every dollar they put in will generate losses, not profits. It's radioactive."

"Like nuclear waste or something?"

She smiled and burst out laughing, looked around one more time, and got serious again.

"No. I mean taxes and the way the city does permits and fees. It would require a massive subsidy just to get the value up to zero."

"That sounds crazy," I blurted out. "Land right downtown, practically on the river, ready for development, is worthless?"

She shrugged. "Under the current system, basically. If a team comes, there will be a ton of money to make the whole thing work. But what if they start building and Portland doesn't get the team? A couple of the big real estate families and other power players have been secretly negotiating – asking for cash up front, a few other things. Then a rumor started going around about another solution: changing the rules for these blocks here and –"

Hannah was waving and pointing again when a brilliant blue-white spotlight swung onto her, lighting her up in the thickening dusk. I swung my head and saw the source: a Lincoln Navigator rolling down Bond Street with headlights like a supernova. A moment later the plasma blinded me and I heard doors open. Reflexively I leaped to the side, out of the beams. When my vision returned all I saw was a large body in dark clothing and an arm swinging at me. I dodged ineffectually and felt thunder in my left temple with enough behind it to knock me off balance. As I started to fall, I swung, my arm glancing off a tight forearm block. I rotated just in time to keep another blow from catching me in the solar plexus. Pain flashed hot and white as I took it in the ribs instead.

Already heading toward the ground, I barely avoided planting face on the deck. Above me, my attacker had moved on. Together with a partner, he was half-dragging-half-carrying Hannah toward the SUV. She twisted and struggled with more power than I'd thought hidden in her tiny frame, actually breaking the hold briefly two times. She started shrieking and screaming "Fire!" at the top of her lungs. I was impressed: someone had taught her what to do in a situation like this and, unlike most people, she managed to do it instead of freezing up.

But the area was mostly deserted and, in the grip of two men, each double her mass, biomechanics was not on her side. One got an arm around her throat for a chokehold. Hannah went silent and a voice, high-pitched for a man, said, "In the car now or we'll tear you apart right here."

She was barely moving as the chokehold tightened. Still on the ground, I pulled my 9mm and lined up the tritium sights. It was no good – Hannah and the man holding her were one dark blob.

"Goddammit!" the man screamed, releasing the hold. Perhaps she had bitten him or managed to stomp an instep or knee his crotch? Steel flashed in the headlight. The second man brought a butterfly knife to the ready and moved in an arc toward Hannah, who was slipping toward the floor.

Three explosions rang out as I fired at the man who'd choked her. Behind the muzzle flash I saw him drop. Knife man let the weapon hit the pavement and turned toward me, reaching inside his jacket. I fired as he drew. His arm came out holding something but by then it didn't matter. I'd put four rounds into the middle of him and he lay on the ground, the silhouette of his gun pointed at the darkening sky.

I dragged myself to my feet as Hannah ran toward me. The door of the Lincoln opened behind her and the driver emerged.

"Fuck! Run!" she said.

Clearly, we were evaluating the situation the same way. We sprinted away from the SUV toward a concrete path and then down to the river. Huddling on a tiny chunk of shoreline called Poet's Beach, we weren't alone. A grizzled man sat nearby, holding something in foil over a tiny fire. My eyes met his. He looked away.

We waited, wrapped in the noisy rush of thousands of vehicles streaming on the interstate, drivers ignorant of our water's-edge drama. We expected the SUV driver to come our way, take a shot at us, or at least point a flashlight in our direction. Minutes went by. Nothing.

I slowly crept up the embankment separating the beach from the hardscaped plaza along the road. Peering over the curb, I saw the driver close the liftgate of the truck, get in front, slam the door, and drive off. He had taken the casualties with him. The road was empty.

10

I climbed down and returned to Hannah at the edge of the beach.

"What's going on up there?" she asked.

"Driver picked up the injured – or the dead – stuffed them in the back of the Lincoln and drove away."

I paused, my face screwed up in curiosity. "You're awfully composed. I do this stuff for a living and, even then, attempted kidnappings and gunfights rattle me to where I try and limit 'em to a couple a year."

"I was Army intel in Kandahar for a bit. I wasn't involved in a lot of real fighting. But surprises from guys with trucks, guns, and bad manners? Everyday part of the job."

The man at the campfire was wide eyed and swigged from a half-pint, then held it out in our direction. I seriously considered it for a second before waving it off. "Thanks, man," I said to him, "but I'm afraid my night's just getting started."

He started to reply but froze before the words came out, raised his hand, and pointed behind me to the river. I followed his gesture. A small craft appeared, motor just audible over the traffic. Suddenly, the boat fired up a blazing spotlight and swung it across the beach. The beam got brighter and bigger. I heard bullets against the rocks of the embankment milliseconds before I heard the report from the weapon that launched them. It was a turkey shoot and if the crew in the Zodiac couldn't hit us from a hundred yards ... well, they'd be at twenty-five yards momentarily. And then on top of us.

The man with the booze vanished into the deepening darkness to the south, out of the floodlight, as Hannah and I ran up the concrete path to the upper bank.

The gunfire ceased. The shooters probably couldn't see us now, and, even in Portland, it would take a lot of guts to shoot blindly upward from the water toward the River Place hotels and condos.

We scrambled westward on Hall, through the driveway of the Douglas Apartments, out the other end into the lot of an abandoned athletic club. Ahead were the remains of a concrete structure – onetime handball courts – effectively a blind alley whose remaining whitewash provided a hazy backstop for bullets that whizzed past, popping and spraying small chunks of cement.

I looked around. The ground floor entryway beneath the athletic club was sealed with chain link topped by coils of razor wire. But someone had cut a man-sized hole in the fencing which we both saw and exploited at about the same moment. Crouched in the blackness, we saw our pursuers approach. They looked at the opening through which we had escaped and stood, speaking to each other for a moment. One of them pulled out a phone and tapped something. Then they walked away back toward the river.

Hannah and I sat in the darkness, waiting.

After about three minutes, she whispered, "This was ... well ... more excitement than I was expecting. I'd better get going. I've got an appointment – " she looked at her phone and then back up, smiling " – in about half an hour with a very cute girl and some good wine."

Despite the revelation about her military experience, I was more perplexed than ever.

"You don't seem entirely shocked by this little adventure tonight."

"Well…"

"Well?"

"That's because … I didn't quite get to telling you before those dickheads pulled up. The only way to make the construction project work is for someone to get a special kind of waiver on a couple of those blocks. It's basically a get-out-of-jail-free card. Ignore the rules even if the baseball team never comes and the stadium never gets built. There's at least two families who've got it clocked and they're trying to make it happen without word getting out. They are aggressive about possible leaks."

"Aggressive like crews with guns?"

"Aggressive like the right words on the right sheet of paper equals a hundred million bucks and comes with a pile of riverfront land to keep in the family forever. So, yeah. Lots of guys with guns."

"You must really trust Amy if you're sharing all this with me."

"Other way. Amy trusts you. Trusting the wrong people gets you killed but not trusting the right ones … same same."

"But the bad guys know where you work."

"Meh. Anyone can find anyone. And they know I'll do my job, process what needs to get processed and I'm still less likely to blab about it than anyone in city hall. These families are in Portland for the long game – generations. Win or lose this deal, they're on to the next one. I'm more worried that we're missing someone."

"Who?"

She stood up, smiled, shook my hand, and said, "No time tonight, but remember there's always another player. Keep your eye on the county and watch out for Oscar."

She turned, strolled out the hole in the chain link fence, and disappeared into the night.

11

I stumbled uphill to the streetcar and rode back to my apartment. There was more research to do and a few things to gather before I could get some sleep. I got as far as the freezer and some gin. The rest of my tasks would have to wait. The drink calmed my nerves too well and I just about stumbled to the bed before blacking out.

The morning found me unmolested despite my neglecting extra security locks before sleep. Sun streamed in and I greedily slurped black coffee as I took my laptop and began a quick run-through of key landowners in the area, especially ones with any connection to the Field Project or the South Waterfront. The biggest parties looked to be the Naylor, Rabson, and Marrenhous families. After that were a couple of LLCs. I tried to take notes but the nice weather made me antsy. I had to get to the Mustang I garaged in northwest and drive down to Yamhill to chat with Fernando's host family, the Owenses.

Before leaving, I packed a gym bag with additions to my first aid kit, five boxes of green tip 5.56 ammo and a stainless 1911 I planned to leave in storage in the country.

I can't afford a house or even a condo the way things have gone in Oregon, let alone anything near the city. But I did manage to get my name on title to a trailer in a charming slice of mobile home park not far from Stag Hollow Creek. It's closer to Yamhill than Newberg but the rent is cheap and the neighbors are solid, even if they wouldn't make a lot of friends this far north on the Willamette. And, underneath that trailer, is a secured metal cache where I collect emergency supplies and store the firearms I don't need in the city.

Now, don't get me wrong. I'm a hell of a lot less worried about the Boogaloo or UN helicopters than I am about the Cascadian subduction zone earthquake. And Yamhill is within walking distance of Portland when the big one strikes. Well, as long as you count a thirty-four mile march, with a backpack full of gear and a brown kitty, as a walk.

I never could get on the same page with some of my neighbors who talked about practicing for a standoff with the feds. But everyone agreed about one thing: Katrina, Covid, the Palisades Fire and the North Carolina floods showed that no matter the party in charge, the almighty U.S. government wasn't coming to save anyone. And, as for the civil servants of the State of Oregon, well, on a good day they'd get as far as a land acknowledgment before tying their shoelaces together and face planting in their own driveways.

Anyway, that's how I found myself spending some time in Yamhill and occasionally enjoying a minor league game. I looked forward to the drive. Although small, puffy clouds were starting to blow in, I expected one of autumn's finer days.

Lugging a backpack and the gym bag, I hopped TriMet out to where I kept the 'stang garaged. Even in the shade, the triple-yellow paint nearly hurt to look at. My grin was a reflex. I tossed everything in the trunk and rolled the beast quietly down the block; I aimed to avoid drawing attention to where I kept her.

Then I swung around to 405 and suffered the freeways and then 99W as far as Tigard before cutting over through wine country. There was a better way to get to Yamhill, if smoother and faster counted as better. But, today, I wanted to work my brain out a little on the puzzles of the case and that seemed to work best when navigating the constant turns, dips, and climbs of the Chehalem Mountains.

Next to Mt. Hood, Mt. Jefferson, or The Sisters, these "mountains" were ant hills. But they made for dramatic and stimulating roads weaving through farms, villages, vineyards, and glades at a pace that induced a compelling state of flow. Twisting the wheel and laying into throttle after each turn, my unconscious slipped entirely free of the grime, the crime, and my sore, aching ribs.

By the time I glided the car through the last few, flat miles along the Yamhill-Newberg Highway, I felt pretty confident of something. I thought back to the warning I'd been given at gunpoint barely twenty-seven hours prior: that a woman would offer me a job with a real estate connection and I'd better not take it. Despite a thematic connection, I was sure that wasn't about Altagracia Nuñez and the kidnapping. The cases, while maybe related, were not the same. And the referenced woman was neither Altagracia nor Hannah.

Beyond that vague conclusion, things became muddier. Was Delany the only connection between the Yamhill Pioneers and the putative Portland major league team? How did Fernando end up involved? How did I earn a breakfast visit from the men in black and who the hell were they working for?

Despite lingering questions, the drive was refreshing in a way that defied words much like the cartwheeling and exploding vigor of the Mustang's 435 horsepower.

12

I pulled off the highway and rolled slowly through the trailer park. Children played in a field near the entrance, but I didn't recognize them. My lot was close to the back, and it didn't look like my neighbors were home. I'd brought Portlandia chocolate from my stash, which I left on their porch – part of a long game to convince them that, contrary to the preachings of a colorful voice on local talk radio, Portland was more than just the abode of the damned.

The interior of my trailer was cool, a pleasant contrast to summer days when I'd arrive to one-hundred-ten-plus. Under the false floor in the living room were the locked and barred panels that hid my cache, a metal box sunk in concrete. I counted ammunition then added the new boxes to the total, placed the .45 on a stand next to the mags, and checked that the dehumidifier rod was still working. I added fresh first aid supplies to a different compartment and checked dates on the old stuff. Then I locked it all back up and headed outside.

Returning to the highway, two farm hands were working on a tractor's engine across the road. I thought I recognized one of them and I pulled off.

"Bill? You still fighting with that engine?" I called out. "Weren't you complaining about it at the saloon two months ago?"

"Jack? Yeah, goddammit. You offering to come over here and help us out?"

"Not sure I'd be much help but if you need another hand…"

"Nah, I'm just fucking with you, Jack. We know what it needs and we got a lot of practice. Every couple days it's the same thing. But we're gonna swap in an overhaul engine end of the season so we just need this one to go a few more weeks."

"Ahright. Good luck, man!"

I saluted and pulled onto the highway. I rolled right through town and out the other side when I got stuck behind a couple of teenagers on ATVs near the church. The ATVs weren't street legal and the kids knew it. I got up onto them quietly and then revved the V8 just for fun. One of the boys almost jumped the curb and I chuckled as they took off in front of me and then out into an empty field past Rowland Creek.

A few more minutes got me to the Owens family home, an ancient, narrow two-story structure with worn and moldy siding in slate gray. I pulled into the gravel driveway, which sloped down alongside the house. The building included a partial basement built into the hill and had a large covered porch at the back, about four feet over my head as I closed the door of the Mustang. Heated voices came from the porch – more than heated, a full blown argument.

I was already showing up unannounced and, not wanting to add intrusion into a family matter to my sins, I called out loudly.

"Sorry to show up right at lunch, but I've got some decent beer if anyone's interested!"

A mixture of voices called back, only one expressing anything like pleasure. I recognized Lenny, extending an invitation to come up the back steps, and his wife Peggy and son Jesse swearing. A fourth, female, voice was unfamiliar.

I hiked up the steps with two four-packs from new east side breweries and landed in the contentious mealtime scene.

Lenny was a tall, thin, muscular man with wavy brown hair just slightly graying. He wore a light flannel shirt and jeans. Aside from a rough shave, he looked put together, just as I'd seen him last. Peggy, on the other hand, seemed to have suffered a bit. Her graying blonde hair was more straight and stringy and in need of a salon. She, too, wore jeans, but had put on a noticeable amount of weight. The biggest shocker was her face: you could see the graceful structure underneath, but her features were puffy and lined and looked as if she'd just stumbled off a fifteen hour redeye flight. Jesse wore a flavor of the broccoli-hair fashion in chestnut brown. He carried a solid, normally friendly face atop a thin neck and slender body. Like so many young adults, though, his mood and fashion choices dominated his appearance. His present agitation stripped the friendliness.

The new and unknown voice had belonged to a pretty, sporty mid-twenties blonde in the sort of pricey athleisure more prevalent near Nike's Beaverton campus. I stuck my hand out.

"Hi! Jack Louis. I ..."

"I almost forgot how hayseed this place was," the girl said, anger melting into sad resignation under Lenny's withering gaze. "Sorry. I'm not sure we've met. Ashley Owens. Been away for a few years."

Peggy filled in the blank. "Ashley is our oldest. She went to school in Los Angeles! She works there as a commercial illustrator."

Mom's pride was palpable, as was Ashley's resurgent anger.

"I don't work there at all!"

"You'll be back, honey. There are other jobs. Everyone changes jobs a lot when they're starting out," her mother offered.

"Not this time. Everyone's gone. Everyone – from all the agencies, not just mine."

Now Lenny weighed in: "I keep telling you, it's just a cycle. Stay tough and you'll be back on top."

"You don't understand what's going on. They still do the work they did a year ago, but it's all AI plus just two tech assistants for the partners. At other shops, a few of the creative directors are still there but everyone else is gone. Like, no one's coming back from that and I'm, like, a hundred thousand in debt from school. I'm going to end up cleaning toilets at a winery or something for the rest of my life." She paused. The table fell silent for a moment. Then she spoke up again, rallying for her final insult. "You ought to know how this goes, dad. When was your last timber job again? Was I even born when the mills closed and they canned all your asses?"

Ashley was white hot, eyes on the verge of tears. Lenny seemingly had the calm of the Buddha. He gently cracked a beer. Perhaps he had heard this speech before. "Ash, I'm doing OK. Stuff happens. That's just how life goes. You can't get angry over –"

Jesse was the son and I knew him well from prior visits. He cut in violently, twenty-two years old now and more fiery than I recalled ever seeing him. "Maybe you fucking should, dad! Maybe you fucking should get angry! Don't you get what's happening? These politicians and ... they ruined your life and now –"

Lenny jumped back in: "Jesse, stop it! Not everything is a conspiracy! Nobody ruined my life. It's not great, but the old forests weren't going to last forever anyway. It was going to end eventually. Might as well save some of it…"

"They would have lasted long enough! Enough for us," Jesse continued. "But they fucked you and you just let them. And then you did all this shit work – gas station, fucking bars, what, now, the oil change outfit? – for years. You said it was for us and so Ashley could go to LA and do commercial art and she did that, she actually did. Remember we visited and she was getting those awards at that place by the beach, that hotel, what was it called? But now they fucked her too. Four years out of school and she's back in Oregon serving rich assholes on vacation. This AI thing, it's just the latest. Can't you see what's going on?"

He didn't wait for an answer, just slowly turned and carried his can of beer down the back stairs. I had come up those stairs about four minutes prior but it felt like an age had gone by.

Peggy turned to me and for a moment I thought she'd spit fire too, but she just looked tired and sad. "I'm sorry, Jack. I'm sorry about all this. The kids… I…"

Her eyes brimmed and tears spilled down her cheeks. I felt awkward as hell. Like I should comfort her, or more like Lenny or Ashley ought to. But they just sat there. Now the silence was as ugly as the shouting had been. Big droplets fell onto Peggy's plate. She looked left and right, as if she was searching for something that wasn't there. Then stood up and walked with her plate and napkin through the doorway into the main house.

Lenny stood up and made the next move. He glanced at Ashley, now sitting, and then at me. "Let's go for a walk, Jack. I can catch you up on a few things. You said in your text that you had questions about Fernando?"

Before I answered, he walked around the table and came up next to me, taking a big swig from his can. He gestured toward the door to the back yard. I opened the door. "This beer is pretty damned great. They're brewing some solid stuff up there in Portland." I followed him down the steps.

13

We walked to the end of the yard and then along a path through a wood.

"Fernando's a great kid. He's been living with us just over a month now. Technically, host families don't exist anymore. But in a lot of places, like here, the players still live with locals. So, legally, he's a tenant like anyone else. We had to spruce up the downstairs room a bit, but it's all pretty chill and we get decent rent for the place, courtesy of the majors. But you must have something specific on your mind?"

I figured I'd jump into the deep end. "Do you have any idea where he is at the moment?"

"Well, he comes and goes on his own, especially in the off season. He was headed to Portland a couple of days ago and we were a bit surprised he wasn't back yesterday – not sure he knows a lot of folks up there – but we figured he was doing something for the team."

"Does he do that often? Do work for the organization that involves going to the city?"

"Not a lot. I mean: when he works with them, it's usually right here in town. But, now that you mention it, he has borrowed Jesse's car a bunch lately. What's going on, Jack?"

"It appears he may have been attacked in the city and that he got away but later disappeared. Possibly kidnapped but it's not completely clear. I've spoken with his mother in the D.R.; she suggested talking to you. At the least you can give me details on the vehicle he was driving."

"Sure," Lenny replied. "That's easy. I've got a copy of the registration somewhere. But, if we can find Jesse, he'll have it in his wallet and you can take a picture right away. Of course, Jesse's not gonna be happy if something happened to the car."

"Thanks. I want to talk to Jesse anyway. Any idea where he'd be?"

"A good bet is right down this way," Lenny gestured down the path. "There's a spot down here where he likes to do some shooting to let off steam. We'd have heard it by now if he was firing, but he might be setting up."

A hundred yards later we emerged from the woods to find Jesse standing at a weathered table reassembling a pistol. He heard us, set down the chunky slide and frame, and turned to Lenny. "Sorry, dad. I guess I'm a bit spicier than I realized today. I'm just hyped about the bar project and pissed about what's happening to Ash. Didn't mean to give you a ton of shit about your stuff too."

"Just be gentle with your mom and with Ash. I promise she isn't looking forward to working here for a single weekend, let alone for a few months. And try not to be so negative. You've got a great thing going on with the saloon."

I started to ask but Lenny read my mind. "Jack would love to hear about that and I'd like to hear the latest too," he said. "But, first, we were wondering if you knew what Fernando went to Portland for. He's run into some trouble and Jack's trying to find him."

Jesse sobered up quickly. "Yeah, he's gone a bunch of times. Some of the owners here have been trying to get involved with a major league team coming to the city. Lots of complicated deals, I guess. Fernando would pick up docs from lawyers here and take them to other lawyers there. Said it was easy money and, anyway, he couldn't really say no to the Pioneers bosses. He borrowed my car."

I jumped in here. "Do you have the details on the car?" Jesse pulled out a registration slip with the year, color, make, model, plate, and VIN and I snapped a pic.

"Wait, something happened to the car?" he asked.

I stretched the truth a little. "It's probably fine, we don't think anyone trashed it or stole it but we want to find it as soon as we can." I looked for an opportunity to change the subject and gestured toward the gun. "What have you got there?"

"It's a pretty sweet 10mm Springfield," he said, pulling the slide onto the frame, snapping the takedown lever, and passing it to me. "Here, want to try?"

He gestured beyond the table, into a cul-de-sac about a hundred feet deep, surrounded on three sides by a grass-covered ridge topped with aspens, their leaves golden in the threadbare autumn sunshine. At the end of the cul-de-sac were target stands with a bullseye and five smaller steel targets in a line. He opened a drawer in the table and pulled out a magazine full of jacketed rounds.

"Why not?" I grinned. "Do you have some ear pro down there?"

Jesse pointed to a shelf under the table with a mess of headsets. We each grabbed one. I snapped the mag into the pistol, bellied up to the table, and put a round downrange. The recoil was more than I was used to.

"Whew! This thing's a bit of a canon, isn't it?"

"You get used to it pretty fast," Jesse replied. "Try again."

I took a breath, and, knowing what to expect this time, slowly squeezed a half dozen shots into a six-inch group at the center of the target.

"You're right," I said. "Not bad at all. And 10mm is enough to seriously end an argument." I smiled. "Maybe I should upgrade and carry one of these. Then again it's a bit chunky."

"Nah, the real problem is moving and shooting – why the FBI gave up on it. Try moving along the firing line and hitting those steel targets."

I gave it a whirl and the kid was right. Once I started moving, and had to bring the weapon back onto different targets and fire quickly, my performance degenerated. After the first hit, I only got one more of the steel targets, the remaining bullets ending up in the backstop. Wrangling this monster would take more practice than I was likely to get.

"Point taken." I laughed, cleared the gun, and handed it back. "A ton of fun, but maybe not a work gun."

It was Lenny's turn to grin. "Unless work involves bears. Jay, you want to take Jack over to the bar and tell him what you're doing there?"

"Sure. I'm gonna finish cleaning this up, and I'll meet you at the house." He started disassembling the weapon again.

As Lenny and I walked back to the house, he filled in some gaps: The Saloon – not the building, but the business – was owned by a Pioneers old-timer who was going off to a retirement home. The man had been working with Jesse on a project to modernize the place, borrow some memorabilia from the owners, set up to sell themed merch to families on game days. Really make a nice, big team spot out of it instead of just a cool old room with cheap beer and wings. Lenny concluded: "He helped Jay get a loan, set up some construction, put him on a path to having a great little business here one day soon."

He talked a lot prouder of his son than the son did of his old man. But then there was a lot Lenny had lived through that Jesse had barely heard about.

14

Back at the house, I sat on the porch and Lenny excused himself to talk to Peggy. He hesitated a moment at the doorway then quietly drifted over to a small corner cabinet, fished a couple of empty liquor bottles from behind the back of it, wrapped them in the loose tail of his shirt, and shuffled into the house.

About a minute later, Ashley appeared with a beer and offered one to me. "Thanks," I said, taking the can and opening it. "Sorry to hear about the job in LA. Technology getting more and more aggressive."

"It was shit timing for me and my friends. Uh, pardon my language. We thought Covid was the worst, just when we were graduating college. But that was nothing when AI came. It went from 'that's a pretty crazy demo' to 'we're all out of a job like for reals' in just three, four years. Jesse yells about it more than I do, but I'm getting a sense of what things must've been like for dad. Jesse used to always be the tough one. Dad called him stoic. At least I'm still young. I'll figure something out... God, who am I kidding? I'm terrified. Can I tell you that, Jack? Don't say anything. But really. I'm fucking terrified."

She scratched at the flaking paint on the dining table. She had Peggy's coloring, but now that stress was coming out, the resemblance became stronger. Tension in the face and lines starting to appear in places Angelenos don't tolerate but Oregonians do. Her terror was a mixture of Gen Z survival anxiety plus a scent of a future in her parents' small town. I couldn't blame her: Portland's and Oregon's fortunes had diverged from those of the Golden State. It wasn't unthinkable that PNW towns would become west coast Appalachia or a rust-belt-style dead end like Buffalo, Flint, Michigan, or Gary, Indiana.

"Aside from the work stuff, has there been any new trouble? With your family or with Fernando and the team?"

Holding the beer can, she set her arm onto the table which gently seesawed: uneven legs on uneven floorboards. "Not really. But you wouldn't know it from the level of fights we've been getting into. Like that scene you walked in on at lunch. Jesse's usually the one to start things. He's been hanging out with some weirdos lately. Y'know, sort of militia types, lots of conspiracy theories…"

"How'd he end up hanging with them? Your dad said things were looking up with a new business and he was busy working on that."

"Oh, yeah. I mean, I'm kind of jealous. If it all works out, it won't just be a local bar anymore. He'll be scooping up some of that fat cash from the wine country tourists, the baseball fans from other towns. There's actually enough there to make a decent living. But he's upset about my situation, kind of pushes his buttons about dad. You saw how angry he gets. And these guys, they're always up for angry. Living in LA, I kinda forgot how many guys around here are like that. The guns and the gear, always threatening something to somebody."

"You wouldn't have any names…?"

"Nah, I only know a couple of first names. Bill someone. John. You better talk to Jesse about that. Looks like he's coming up from the back now."

Jesse appeared at the door and presently walked through. Ashley took her beer and silently left in the other direction. Jesse looked calmer, more cleaned up, cheerful, and put together than earlier; he looked like the young man I'd met prior to today.

"So, Jack: I'm going over to do a little work on the bar. Do you want to come take a look? The new toys are hidden in the back so far, but it's pretty sweet. I remembered a couple more things Fernando said, too. Not sure if they're useful…"

I accepted and offered him a ride then said quick goodbyes to the rest of the family. Exiting via the back steps, we hopped in my car and I drove across town to the saloon by the ballpark.

15

In contrast to game days, the block was empty and the bar nearly so. The place smelled of old wood, malt, popcorn, cool sticky air. In addition to light from the windows, narrow, irregular shafts of sunlight blasted in through cracks and gaps in the wooden facade. A closer look revealed thick layers of glass or plexiglass and an air gap covering the old timber facing and sealing the interior against extreme heat or cold. But the transparent materials preserved a curious old-fashioned illumination; it felt a bit like stepping into a barn. Of course, there were also electric lights deeper in the place for practical purposes.

Two men at a corner table near the stage wore suits and murmured to each other over burgers and beers. A woman in work clothes was the only one at the bar, where she sipped a drink and tapped at her phone.

Behind the bar was a freckled kid with coarsely executed wet mop hair, dirty blond, whose face was somehow slightly off and who almost looked too young to be serving booze. As soon as we walked through the door, Jesse called out to him. "Tyler! How's it going, man? Everybody behaving theirselves today?"

The kid cheerfully replied, "All good, boss!"

"Tyler, this is Jack Louis, a friend of my parents. He came from Portland to poke around after Fernando." Turning to me, he waved toward the barman. "Jack, Tyler. Best bud forever and soon to be my first employee. Tyler's thinking about partnering with me, buying a chunk of the place from old Reggie. You've been here before, right? But I bet you never noticed – look at that case over there."

He gestured to the far end of the bar.

"That's Reggie's bat from when he won the Upper West Championship with a grand slam for the Pioneers. And his jersey is on the wall behind it. I know, you can barely see it. Reggie's a local legend but he never did that much with this place. That's all gonna change. By next spring, I'm gonna have it redecorated, we'll have a ton of memorabilia on loan from the team, I'm gonna have this whole section in the front for selling merch – it'll open onto the sidewalk and we'll make a mint on game days. The old hero's been helping me. Plus Fernando and a few other guys on the team. George Delany helped me get a loan, can you believe that?"

The kid was firing on all cylinders now.

"Not much to see yet, but come in the back. I've got all the new sound gear for when we have music. New mics and PA already set up, and check this out."

He walked to a doorway in the rear, behind the stage, motioning for me to join him. As we passed through, he turned left into a dark room like a large pantry. I followed and he closed a door behind us, flipping on a light. "It's like a recording studio in here!" I exclaimed.

"Not quite," he corrected. "But it's top notch for what it is. I came down today because Tyler said we got one more panel delivered. This box here. I figured I'd hook it up."

He unpacked the box and moved a bunch of cables around. A few minutes later, he said, "Let's test 'er out.

Here, turn that light off – then we can look out this window over here onto the stage."

I complied and we could see the empty stage and nearly empty bar. There was a new arrival, a thirtyish redhead in curls seated against the wall with a laptop open. The men in suits were chattering. I heard a pop as Jesse worked some switches. Then a quiet male voice emerged from the monitors.

"It'll be right here. Apartments, townhouses, and a B&B at the end of the block. See, even if they keep operating the team, it's too close to Portland, they won't leave it here, they'll have to move it – Medford, Bend, somewhere farther away."

Jesse had a puzzled look when I glanced over, but he didn't say anything. He twisted a dial and another voice came out, a bit louder this time.

"I get that part but what if Portland doesn't get the team? Then what?"

The first man responded, "It's gonna work out either way. In that case, we'll flip the piece in the city and the option alone is enough to do the whole development here, easy."

The second man looked around, laughed, and said, "I'll miss this place."

The first man stood, his chair rendering an awful scraping sound though the speakers. "Shut the fuck up," he laughed. "You've been here, what, once a year for an ownership meeting? I'm pretty sure you'll be fine back in LA."

The other man put on sunglasses and said something but the mics didn't pick it up as the pair grabbed their paperwork and half-empty beer glasses and walked away.

Acting on impulse, I told Jesse to stay in the booth. I opened the door, turned the corner, and emerged into the barroom in time to see the redhead walk across the mens' path. The man with the sunglasses jumped back and to the side; the other plowed into her, spilling beer and dropping a folder of notes and printouts. The woman squatted instantly, and scooped up the papers while apologizing.

"Don't worry about it," the man said, taking the folder back from her. The men headed out the door as Tyler came over with a bar towel to wipe up the floor.

"You OK?" I asked the redhead.

"Oh. Yes. I can't believe I did that," she said, retreating to her table and laptop.

I lowered my voice and leaned in. "I can. That was a pretty slick move. Want to tell me what it's all about?"

"Well, what makes you so curious?" she began.

I gave her my best smile, which was still pretty mediocre. "Gotta stay curious, right?"

"Read my blog. 'On the Waterfront PDX' it's called." She stuck out a hand. "Abby Sparrow. I've got an article about all this coming out in a few days."

I shook the hand and introduced myself.

She gave me a nicer smile than I deserved, flipped her laptop shut, and headed for the exit. I wasn't sure what she knew, but, if she knew anything, I wasn't sure that blogging about it was a bright idea. "Hold on," I called after her. "I might have something important for you before you write up your piece."

Abby hesitated then said, "OK. I gotta run now. Call me," and reached into her purse, handing me a precut slip of paper containing her name, an email address, a phone number, a QR code, and a URL. Then she turned and rushed out the door.

Tyler stood up with the bar towel and grinned. "Right on. She's pretty cute. A bit old for me. But hey, gotta love a MILF." The grin got bigger and became almost a leer. Something was slightly off about Tyler but I ignored that and asked if he knew Abby or the two men in suits. "Nope, never seen 'em before."

"Is it unusual," I asked him, "for people to come in dressed up and talking business here?"

"Not really, at least not on weekday afternoons. Makes a way better place for a meeting than the Starbucks or that other coffee place they got in Newberg." He emitted an awkward laugh.

Jesse had emerged from the back and called out, "What the hell was that whole meeting about?" He seemed to be on the verge of getting fired up once again.

I kept my suspicions to myself. "Just a couple of rich assholes drinking and talking trash. I wouldn't worry about it," I lied.

Jesse relaxed and seemed to accept my assertion, then leaned over to me, tensed up and spoke with a voice that had dropped ten decibels and a couple of octaves. "I swear to God, this place gets screwed up, I'm gonna lose it. Some friends have been tryin' to warn me off, said we're screwed even in towns like this, between the Democrats, Jews, Chinese buying up the land–"

I put an arm on the kid's shoulder to soften the interruption, but had to cut him off. "You have friends here saying that?"

"Well, I guess. Around here. In Oregon, anyway. We hang out online and talk shit. Sometimes I think they're joking, but they say it's never been this bad and stuff is ready to go off."

I thought for a moment before responding. "Well, I was on the east coast when 9/11 happened. Towers came down in New York, planes stopped flying, then the anthrax and the highway shooters. I think the world's always pretty crazy so just ... be careful who you're hanging out with. Maybe spend some more time with your sister. And Tyler, here."

He didn't have a quick response to that, which I took to be a good sign. I wanted to burnish his ego a little, so I said: "It sounds like half the town has your back taking over this place here. It's gonna be fantastic and I can't wait to come back and see it."

I headed toward the door, calling out: "I got a couple of leads to chase down tonight. And maybe I can even wrangle a date with that redhead."

Tyler chimed in with an overdone, "Aww yeah!"

"Just text me if you guys find out anything about Fernando."

Heading to my car, I realized I hadn't eaten anything since a couple of protein bars back in my trailer. My thoughts were unclear. What were the odds of finding Abby before she got back to Portland? Any chance she'd answer a call or a text? She might have information. She might have information that could get her hurt. I sat silently in the Mustang, taking in the musky leather and plasticizer as the sky began to darken.

16

A wreck dissuaded me from Tualatin Valley Highway and fatigue kept me out of the wine country hills. Instead, I headed toward Newberg and a slog up 99 after that. Around Newberg, I decided to give Abby a call. She picked up right away.

"Jack Louis here. I'd really like to talk to you about your article and the men we saw in Yamhill. I'm not a journalist, activist, blogger, podcaster, anything like that. I'm doing a private investigation into a disappearance. And there's a chance those men might be connected with it somehow."

"Are you, like, actually a detective?" she asked. There was disbelief; I wasn't sure if "mock" ought to qualify the disbelief or not.

"For real. I have ... well, not a badge, but a little plastic card from DPSST. They do certification for –"

She interrupted me. "I know what DPSST is. I also know their licenses are public record, so I'm gonna look you up. But I'll give you a sneak preview of what I'm working on just because it's gonna light up the town when it comes out. Swear you won't scoop me or blab on social media ... and did I mention I'm gonna look you up?"

"Yeah, I got it sister."

"Be nice. Now, where to start. Hmm. So, have you ever heard of a thing called the Portland Field Project?"

"Yes, the org trying to get a Major League Baseball team in –"

"What the fuck?!" she interrupted again, aggressively.

"What's going on? Was that meant for me?"

"Sorry, Jack," she resumed. "This asshole keeps riding up right behind me and flashing his brights. His lights are high and it's blinding me. And it's super rude." She took a deep, audible breath. "OK, so the Field Project needs – Shit! This guy's practically hitting me. Why doesn't he just go arou – oh there's a car there."

"Where are you?" I asked.

"About a mile past Newberg. Must be some country guys being dickheads. Shit! Jack, the car to my left, someone is shining a super bright flashlight into my car and I'm stuck."

"Is there anyone in front of you? Can you go faster?"

"Not really. I'm rocking a Honda Fit and it can't outrun a truck or a BMW."

"OK, hang up and call 911. They'll get your position. And you'll be in the suburbs near Sherwood in a few minutes. Don't stop, go straight to the Sherwood police station, it's right off 99. Take a left at the medical center. Stay safe and let me know you got there."

"I'll try." She disconnected.

As I left Newberg, I stomped it and heard the roar of the V8 as the Mustang leaped forward into the night. I glanced at the speedometer. Hell, I thought, the OSP is never around when you need 'em anyway. At this rate, I'd be in Sherwood in a couple of minutes.

The phone rang through the hands-free system and I reflexively eased off the gas as I answered.

"Jack!" Abby's voice was frantic. "You know the Cedar Creek Diner?"

"Yeah, I'll be passing it in like thirty seconds."

"Stop there. Please. You'll see me when you walk in."

Questions flooded my mind but I figured they'd get answered soon enough. "OK, I'll be there in a minute."

17

I started to slow as I approached the curve that hid the diner. As it appeared in view, my headlights caught a Honda Fit off the side of the road, angled and pitched down from the highway toward the creek. Just a hundred yards farther was the diner. I parked and walked toward the giant illuminated "Cedar Creek Diner and Sports Bar" sign with a reader board underneath proclaiming PRIME RIB SATURDAY NITES. KARAOKE FRI & SAT 9 PM. A complementary neon sign reinforced that the place was OPEN and three long strings of Jack-o-Lantern Halloween lights warned of further kitsch inside.

Upon entering, I found myself looking down a bar running along one side of the place. On the other side were pinball machines and, in between, high-top cocktail tables. A bit farther in, there were two unmarked steps down to a lower restaurant seating area. The lighting wasn't bright. I imagined the two steps generated extra beer sales by way of drunken spills but would end up drawing a lawsuit when something more important than a pint glass hit the floor. Abby sat at a table in the far corner. As I advanced, a man – possibly waiter, cook, and owner – converged on us from the opposite direction.

He placed two menus on the table and, before he could ask or tell us a thing, Abby said, "Vodka rocks. Double. Please." He looked in my direction. "Gin martini. Olives," I said, and he quickly rattled off a list of brands. I named a local distillery out of Albany and the man nodded and left.

I didn't have to ask Abby the obvious question.

"I tried to call 911," she began, "but the lights were in my face and I hit a pothole or something. My phone went flying. The truck was right up behind me. I think he might have bumped me but I'm not sure. And the passenger in the other car, the BMW, was shining this super bright light in my face and I think I saw a gun. I remembered what you said: just keep driving, only a few minutes to the cops in Sherwood. But that spot where the road curves – you know, just before you get here? – those guys kept going straight and ran me off the road. I couldn't turn. Then the curb came up and I went into the gravel. Luckily there was a lot of space. I rolled along until the gravel ran out and came to a stop in the grass."

"And the truck? The car?" I asked.

"They went blasting on by. As soon as I was off the road, they turned and drove away like nothing happened. I think my car's OK, actually. I probably could still drive it, but I was so freaked out. I found my phone, and saw the light from this place right up ahead so I came here and called you while I was walking. At first, I thought it was a couple of drunk rednecks hassling me because of my tiny car and vegan bumper stickers. That shit I can deal with, though. I don't know what this was."

"I might have an idea. If you can tell me what was up with the two men in Yamhill, maybe I can put it together."

"One of those guys is Joseph Bunton, he's well known in Salem, represents various business interests. He runs an LLC called Summer Fun, which owns a big chunk of the

Pioneers. The other guy is either his lawyer or accountant, he's from California. I think Bunton, or the other members of the company, are planning to bail out of the Pioneers and invest in development near a future ballpark in the city. What I don't understand, though, is how they expect to end up with so much money out of the deal that they can build this other crazy big development in Yamhill as well. You'd think it was the other way around: they won't get much selling a stake in a minor league team and the Portland development is, pardon the pun, big-league pricey."

Flashes of light here and there in the back of my consciousness flickered but didn't connect. It was like I could feel a spark of thought and willed it to blossom without success. I gave up and went back to basics:

"I thought George Delany was the majority owner of the Pioneers and he's a local right in Yamhill."

"George is the *biggest* owner, but he's not a *majority* owner. He owns a bit more than a third. The next biggest investor is some LLC with investors all over. It's incorporated here in Oregon so it's easy to see their info and it's boring as hell. Then there's Summer Fun LLC and a few tiny individual investors, mostly well-to-do locals. Summer Fun is the wildcard. It's set up in Nevada so info is hard to come by. But Bunton and his associates are old-school Oregonians with sketchy connections going back forty years."

"And how did you get into all of this?"

"Anything getting built by the rivers in Portland, I write about it. The stadium is – potentially – big news. I didn't have a lot of expectations when I started researching. But something's up. I don't get how all of this money is flying around when the team may not even come to Portland and the stadium may never get built. Plus: all the biggest downtown buildings are empty, in foreclosure, or both. Who the hell is financing anything new? In the bar, I really wanted a look at the papers Bunton and his friend were looking at. I've got a photographic memory so…"

She smiled. I smiled back. "What did you see?" I asked her. As she opened her mouth to answer, out of the corner of my eye I spotted someone slowly approaching from the kitchen – the waiter with our drinks, I guessed.

"Legalese – I'll have to write it out and ask AI what it all means. Can't afford a real lawyer. But George Delany's name was all over the two docs I saw."

The man reached our table. Before I could say anything else to Abby or thank him for the drinks, I realized he wasn't the waiter and he wasn't carrying a tray. He was holding a carbine across his waist – until he flipped the stock up and slammed a metal buttplate solidly into the side of my head and everything went black.

18

The sensation that returned first was cold. Icy and really sticky, like my face was glued to something. My eyes eventually opened on an incoherent sight. Illuminated and shiny everywhere but dim and hard at the same time. I tried to pick up my head and it felt like my face was tearing off. I reached up expecting to feel blood. I couldn't feel anything at all – my fingers were numb.

The tip off was an enormous corrugated carton with a Tillamook Ice Cream logo. I was in a walk-in freezer, and the fact that I was thinking at all meant I couldn't have been in here long.

Turning slowly around, I saw metal racks filled with more cartons, some labeled beef or pork, others torn open to reveal chicken patties, fries, cutlets, and other short-order cooking staples. It appeared I'd been lying on a crushed and torn box which was covered in blood. Then I saw Abby, in the corner, slumped against the wall. She was breathing – you couldn't miss puffs of steamy breath in the icy air. But neither of us would be breathing for long if we didn't get out.

I pushed the safety release plunger in the door and felt a little movement but I couldn't get the door to open. The unit had an alarm button so I tried that and heard the piezoelectric whine of a buzzer somewhere outside the freezer. While waiting for a response, I pulled Abby up from the metal walls and floor, which would conduct heat away from her body even faster than the air. She showed tiny signs of consciousness but couldn't support herself so I dragged some cartons together, tried to make a sort of chair and ended up leaning her into a messy cardboard pile instead.

I didn't have my phone and – so far as I could tell without an excessively intimate search – neither did she. My watch was still on, however. It was just after 7:30 p.m., so there ought to be people in the restaurant hearing the alarm. After a few more minutes, I got impatient, moving boxes and shoving empty shelves around, hoping the exertion would keep me less frozen, when I caught a glimpse of red behind a carton of fish. Yanking the box out of the way, I saw a fireman's axe mounted to the wall. I grabbed it.

The axe head was large and had a massive awl on the opposite side. I drew it back to swing – but what exactly to hit? The door latch wasn't the problem since the emergency release had worked. The rest of the hardware – hinges, latches, whatever, must be on the outside.

An awful shriek cut through the icy air. I twisted halfway around to see Abby, sitting up and staring at me holding the axe. I slowly set it down. "I'm just trying to get us out of here."

"Oh god! Your face!"

"What?" I asked reflexively.

"What happened?" she half-yelled, hysterical at seeing me with God-knows-what sort of injury swinging an axe in this dimly lit frigid prison.

"I don't know exactly. We were talking, I could see the whole front of the dining room so someone must have come in from the back and clocked us. Based on the food here," I gestured at the boxes, "we're probably still in the diner. Door and alarm did nothing, so now I gotta find something to chop."

"The wall over there, next to the door."

"What? Just ... beat on the flat metal wall?" I asked, incredulous.

"Yep! It's not a bank vault. These things are mostly made of styrofoam."

I looked at her like she was nuts but took a big swing at the wall. The axe sliced through the sheet metal and deep into something flimsy underneath.

"What the hell?" I spontaneously blabbed.

To which Abby replied with a groan, "I've worked in a lot of restaurants and walkins. Never been locked in one before, but we used to talk about it all the time. You keep chopping, detective man."

A few more strokes and there was a decent sized hole to the outside. Between kicking and swinging, I made a hole big enough for us to squirm out of.

No tropical beach could ever feel as warm and heavenly as the eighty-degree kitchen after an hour plus in the ice box.

19

We had been leaning against steel prep tables just breathing – and wondering why we seemed to be alone in the place – for a good five minutes, when Abby said, "You better take a look at your face."

I found a sink with a mirror and saw a bunch of blood and long strips of what appeared to be skin. I recoiled at the reflection before realizing it wasn't skin: it was cardboard. Apparently, I had bled a decent amount and the blood had frozen my face to a carton. When I got up, slices ripped off the box and remained frozen to my bloody face and now it was all melting, which produced a hideous appearance. I began laughing when I realized what Abby must have experienced when she came to in the freezer and saw me with a face like this, swinging a yard-long axe. After a quick rinse in the sink, I looked less wretched.

In the mirror, Abby came up behind me. "There's someone in the closet."

She led me to a locked wooden door. Thumping and slight grunting noises were audible behind it. I returned to the axe, drew it back, called out, "Heeeere's Johnny!" and smashed open the top part of the door. Through the gap it was possible to see two people thrashing around on the floor.

A bit more work got the door open. We untied the restaurant owner (our cocktail waiter) along with a teenage cook (apparently the owner's son) and removed tape from their mouths. There were chunks of dried blood on the backs of their heads, where they said they'd been slugged.

We all awkwardly apologized to each other – they for allowing us to be attacked in their store, we for accidentally drawing in guys who roughed them up. They were calling the cops but I started heading for the exit. I could do a statement later but didn't feel like hanging around here any longer. Abby caught up to me at the front door where we found the fake neon "OPEN" sign unplugged, the "Closed" placard flipped around and, most importantly, the door locked. Which explained the lack of customers.

I offered Abby a ride with me back to Portland, pointing out that we had no phones now and the troublemakers were still out there. She said if she was able to get her car back on the road, she'd rather head home on her own. She was, and she did.

The Mustang was still where I'd left it and it got me back up 99W. I stopped at a grocery in Tigard so I could stumble around and grab a rotisserie chicken and a beer for dinner. I got on the freeway, took that to the Everett Street exit, and chanced parking outside my building, since I was too tired to go to the garage and back.

I was walking to my entrance past the door to El Dorado when Logan looked up from a conversation with his bouncer and caught a glimpse. I held up a hand – half greeting, half "don't even say it" and he just slowly shook his head. Pretty sure he was wearing a bit of a grin, too.

Upstairs, I cracked the beer and got through about a quarter of the chicken before I stumbled to the bed and passed out.

20

I guess the clubbing on the head and the visit to the freezer weren't that bad, because I woke up about 6 a.m. feeling pretty good. I reached for my phone and remembered … that I didn't have a phone. Well, if the bad guys weren't smart enough to isolate the phone with a Faraday bag, I might be able to track it. I popped open my laptop. The device appeared instantly and I'm not sure if I was glad or disappointed to see it was at the police station in Sherwood. Probably glad. While I wouldn't have minded an excuse to track the asshole who whacked me – and to be suitably prepared this time – there were more pressing tasks.

The Mustang had survived the night with no damage beyond a big splat of birdshit on the otherwise pristine yellow roof. The whole car looked duller than usual in an autumn fog that lay in the flats all along the river and up against the west hills.

My head was OK, the car was OK, and my phone was OK. I decided to exploit the circumstance and retrieve the phone immediately.

At the station, I became a minor celebrity: the diner attack was pretty exciting for the area. Relevant officers were reached by phone and agreed to forego an interview. An evidence tech pulled out my phone but wouldn't let me have it until a records guy watched me fill out a form and then dictate more details into a computer. I read everything over and signed it then took my phone and rolled to a nearby drive-through coffee hut.

I sat in my parked car letting the brew cool and emailed Abby to say that her phone was probably also with the cops. I'd asked them; they had hinted but not officially confirmed it.

Then I played a voicemail that had arrived overnight from a number I didn't recognize. It was Peggy Owens and she was frantic.

Per Peggy, Jesse had been in his room around eleven when he came downstairs fuming about "rich assholes" shutting down the Pioneers and destroying his business. He'd launched into a rant about people ruining America and something about guys online calling Tyler a retard. Then he stormed off into the night saying he needed to work some things out.

Peggy said she figured he'd just hang out with his friend and play video games or drive around to let off some steam. That he'd stay over at a friend's if he didn't come home to sleep. But now she was worried. She'd looked in his room and a bunch of stuff was gone including an expensive rifle normally locked in a wood-and-glass display case. Now he wasn't answering his phone.

She asked me to call her back. I would, but I needed a little more caffeine in me first. Once I had consumed sufficient coffee and gotten on the road back to Portland, I rang her but was unable to learn nor share any useful info. I calmed her down a bit, I think, reminding her that it was entirely plausible Jesse had just gone shooting in the woods to cool off. My friends and I had done similar stuff at that age. Technically, we didn't have as much in the way of weapons or woods where I grew up, so we ended up doing even more dangerous and foolish things instead. Anyway, I told her it all came with the testosterone and he'd be OK. I mostly believed it.

In King City, I pulled off to tank up and, while the attendant pumped, I looked at my phone and found another message from Abby. She had already figured out where her phone was – I think she was hinting that journalists know how to find things too – but she thanked me for the info and for the help the previous night. She also said if I was coming up I-5 into the city, I might want to look for smoke. One of her sources had tipped her off about a car bombing in the South Waterfront. A followup message with a large monocle-face emoji reinforced the subtle suggestion that she was a step ahead of me.

I collected the receipt for my gas and headed north.

21

The Mustang made noise tearing up the freeway but it still took twenty minutes to reach the South Waterfront. Any smoke was long gone. Nevertheless, curiosity led me in the direction of the condo towers on the river. Turning north on Bond, I rolled slowly, looking for any sign of emergency vehicles.

I got almost to the hospital before sparkling lights hit me from the right. The parking lot east of OHSU was, apparently, a crime scene. Two trucks from Fire and Rescue along with two police SUVs were arranged in the lot around the charred corpse of a vehicle.

The road was closed off, so I parked and hoofed over. With luck, one of the cops there would recognize me and casually fail to notice as I milled around snooping.

No luck. I was intercepted – by firemen – before I could get a good look. Plan B was a camera with an absurdly long lens. The camera was often Plan B, so it lived in a Pelican case in the trunk of the Mustang. I had to reposition the car a couple of times but eventually got a photo of the burnt license plate. The plate bore a few legible characters and hung on the remains of a Mercedes AMG S-Class, a daily driver in New York or California but practically on par with a Lamborghini in PDX. In the background was a van with the Multnomah County logo on it and a partially obscured placard. What I could see read, "SERVICES CO-

ORDINATION AND RESPONSE," a bureaucratic mouthful I'd have to look up later.

Photos would have to do it for now, so I left and took the 'stang to its stable in northwest. Not having an office to set up in was starting to grate. Not having a decent breakfast was grating as well so I took TriMet to Agamemnon's Tavern on Burnside.

The tavern was a robustly fortified wooden space occupying the ground floor of a building about as far from modern city code as Portland was from Grants Pass.

While the tavern might have been too bright to nurse a hangover, it was otherwise a cool, empty and cheap spot to start thinking for the day. It also let me skip the unappealing breakfast options at home. I tore at an omelette and opened my laptop. An obvious next step was to identify the destroyed car, but I didn't even get that far.

None of my databases had anything on the license plate. Perhaps the car's owner was law enforcement? There were also a few other, more exotic, possibilities.

Frustrated and impatient, I texted Amy at Jeff Spencer's office and asked if she could help me find anything. After a few minutes, she texted and told me to ask Hannah. Hannah was easy to get on the phone, as she held a city job. But before I could even get to the details, she interrupted: "Oh, yes, I remember we were going to talk about that at your friend's party. I'm pretty busy at work, but we can sync on my cell in a few. Bye!" and hung up.

I didn't have her cell.

Ninety seconds later, my phone buzzed and Amy sent me a text containing the letter "H" and a number.

What the hell, I thought, and dialed it. Hannah picked up immediately.

"Hey, that was slick," I said. "Thanks for sharing your number. I guess there were a lot of people around at work and it wasn't a great place to chat?"

"It's not so much that," she answered, "as the fact that what you're looking for is outside of my access as a city employee. But... hmm..."

She verbally hesitated for a moment and then went quiet. I've found that the best followup question is often silence. So I tried some myself and it worked.

She spoke up: "The thing is... I have a couple of side gigs for other agencies that the city doesn't know about. And ... I do them all at the same time, but have to keep the data trails separate."

"I'm just grateful for the help," I said. But I couldn't help adding, after a moment, "I suspected there was more to you than met the eye the other night. Not, er, that I'm complaining about what met the eye..."

"Great. That's cute. I'll see what I can dig up."

I figured I got off lightly for Portland.

Sitting there, as my lava-hot black coffee blistered its way through my palate, I began worrying about Jesse. He was more volatile than he'd seemed when I'd met him before. Maybe just growing pains, but he was an adult now, if young. Online chat rooms with Oregon good ol' boys were one thing, but running off with a rifle when you realize the world's currents might just flow in and knock you on your ass ... that was a big step in a dark direction.

Jesse was classic Oregon: proud, volatile, idealistic, anxious, and wary of outsiders. Pioneer ethos had imbued the state with a mixture of self sufficiency to the point of radical libertarianism, trust in almost no social institutions, and reliance on natural resources as the ultimate currency … all tempered by neighborly tolerance and a dash of nineteenth-century American utopianism. How well that brew would serve in the twenty-first century was as yet unclear.

My phone's buzz interrupted my rumination.

22

"The car belongs to Isabelle Delany. Local cops and OSP have not yet determined who was inside. One body was recovered." Hannah spoke in a quiet monotone.

"OK, got it."

"Don't hang up!"

"OK..."

"It might be the case that Isabelle was not in the car and that she is alive."

"Yeah, I understand that's a possibility."

"You're not listening. It might be the case that she was not in the car, that someone else was placed in the car..."

"OK, I get it."

"Oh my god for a genius private eye or whatever Amy calls you – you know she holds you in quite high regard, right? – you're dense as a brick today. It might be that Isabelle has some information you could use and that she might need your help. She might be at the bar in The Portland City Grill at 4 p.m. and the service elevator might be the best way to get there."

The extra pint of coffee was slowly kicking in for me. "And," I said, "it might be the case that the service elevator access is open somewhere in Big Pink?"

"God I hope I never end up as old as you," Hannah said.

"Hey!" I shot back, slightly hurt.

"OK, OK. You're catching on. Take the stairs to three and find the access to the service elevator."

"Thanks," I said, with a tiny bit of sarcasm. "Is that it?"

"Is that it? That's a lot of info that ... none of the locals have. Officially, that no one has. You're welcome. In fact, I feel like you owe me something." A bit of playfulness crept into her voice. I played back.

"Owe you something? Didn't I shoot someone for you a couple of days ago? I might have killed him for all I know."

"Yeah, that was on me. I should have been better prepared for those guys. Oh, and you didn't kill him."

"How do you…?" I started to ask. "Never mind, I get it. Thanks. If someone wanted to compensate someone else in a friendly manner for their help…?"

"I'll text you," she said and hung up.

The speculative plan to look for Isabelle at City Grill left me most of the day to worry about other tentacles of the case waving wildly in space, anchored to nothing.

Absent a better idea, I tried Jesse's phone. I was surprised when he picked up right away. He was willing to talk; better than that, to meet; and, best, not too far away. The cops had released his car – the one Fernando had brought to Portland – and he was on his way into town to grab it at a tow lot under I-405. The connection was noisy as hell: apparently, Jesse had hopped on the 150cc dirt bike he and Tyler were working on and he was riding it to Portland a long (and not entirely legal) way through the country.

As long as he stayed off the interstate, and didn't get unlucky running across an OSP trooper in a bad mood, he'd get away with it and probably get to the lot within an hour.

I paid and started a leisurely walk up Nineteenth hoping for further inspiration with a detour around Couch Park. A rich bounty of trash, including foil, needles, and less discrete biohazards assailed my senses. In the rhetoric of the pure and distant turnip eaters, I reminded myself, these artifacts served merely as the most recent totems of urban weakness and corruption.

Here, grounded in reality, there was a citizen group, an organized patrol, surrogates for the understaffed absent police, attempting to attenuate the park's filth and secure it for the schoolchildren who crossed each day. The group's risky and thankless work was opposed by an oddball club of dedicated chaos agents dumping syringes and supplies to attract trouble like breadcrumbs for pigeons.

A few minutes later, I arrived at the tow lot awkwardly squeezed under the freeway. With no sign of Jesse, I relaxed against a concrete post to wait. It was still early enough in the autumn that the fog was beginning to lift, burn and blow off in late morning sun.

There was still enough fog, however, to create a terrifying cinematic scene as a dark figure emerged from a distant blur, approaching on a motorbike with a growling whine. The breeze blew dead leaves and paper bags against the curb. Scraps of food wrappers swirled, occasionally sticking to the wet filth in the road as the bike drew closer and the rider's silhouette resolved. A shadow in motocross gear emerged and became a man, a rifle strapped to his back.

I experienced deja-vu waiting for the recollection to click: I was watching a low-budget Portland remake of Schwarzenegger's legendary scene from *The Terminator*. Arnold, of course, wore leather, carried a shotgun, rode a

Harley-Davidson Fat Boy and looked a hell of a lot cooler doing it ... but I had to give Jesse a nod as he pulled up and took the helmet off.

"What the hell is up with the gun? Isn't that a bit much?" I asked.

"Hey, you don't have to be an asshole," Jesse replied. "It's an open carry state."

Despite not being a father, I couldn't help launching into dad mode: "Just because it's legal doesn't mean it isn't idiotic. You could get yourself killed."

"By who?" he shot back. "By the cops? Not here in Portland, they're a bunch of pussies. And where I live, the cops are all used to seeing it."

"Yeah, how about some civilian who gets terrified when you blast in here and freaks out. Or an enforcer for one of the drug gangs, maybe thinks you're playing where you shouldn't be or – worse – that you want to lighten his backpack?"

Jesse was about to yell something when he stopped and took a breath. "Shit. Yeah, OK. I didn't think about that. I wasn't coming prepared for a fight. I do have body armor for when the shit goes down but I'm not wearing it today. Just want my damned car back. Here," he said, taking off his backpack and pulling an empty canvas duffle bag out of it. "We can put the gun in along with this stuff." He pulled off the jacket and gloves and stuffed them, together with the helmet and gun, into the duffle. "Better?"

"Much," I said. "Let's go to the gatehouse and see about getting your car. You sure it's in this lot?"

"Yeah, I had to look on the city's website and then another site to find it. I keep one of those location trackers in the car all the time, just in case, but when I looked for it, it showed in the middle of some building. I guess someone stole it when the whole thing went down with Fernando."

We presented the paperwork and cash to an attendant who punched some buttons on a computer, disappeared for a minute, and came back with a receipt and a set of keys.

"Right over here," Jesse said, smiling and leading me to a roughly decade-old Mazda MX-5 Miata. The car was dirty as hell and had a few scratches but, underneath the filth, I could see pearlescent red paint. It had a stick – which also meant it had the beefier engine. This car would be a blast to drive and probably look damned good after a wash and detail. Jesse got inside and started the engine.

"Pretty sweet," I said to him. "What are you going to do with your bike?"

"Figured I'd lock it up and leave it here, maybe come back later and get it with somebody's truck."

"Want to lock it behind my place? I've got a little space we can put it … and if you'll come log onto my computer so we can see where your location tracker went, I'd really like to find out who's got it. That might be a clue to finding Fernando."

"Hell yeah!" Jesse said. I gave him my address and he revved the engine and tore out of the parking lot.

I took the dirt bike which – like pretty much any dirt bike – was also a blast, at least for the five minutes it took to pull up at the side of my building. Jesse was already there, looking like the cat that ate the canary in his Miata.

Upstairs, as I opened my computer, he kept walking around the place in circles, like he expected there to be more to it. "Is there another floor or some more rooms? Maybe a garage or a workshop? You must go crazy in here," he said.

"Nah, and anyway I got that trailer down in the country near your folks," I reminded him. "For when I really need a break from the insanity."

After he logged into his cloud account and picked the device to track, we were looking at a slice of downtown not far west of where we were sitting. A pulsing blue dot appeared in the middle of a mixed-use building.

"Let's go!" I declared and headed for the door, carrying the laptop with me.

"Like, right now? We're just going to go there? What are you gonna do?" Jesse asked.

"I'll figure it out." He was unpredictable but, in the moment, I needed his car or his bike. "I could use your help. Come on."

We raced downstairs, got into the Miata, and I gave directions from my screen while Jesse drove. I had him slow down and park two blocks from the target. I handed him a steering wheel immobilizer I'd found under the passenger seat and subtly gestured toward three vagrants arguing and throwing bottles against a wall at the end of the block.

We locked up and walked toward a gray concrete five-over-one with "The Cascadia" emblazoned in vinyl decals on its ground-floor windows.

"Just stay chill and let me do the talking," I told Jesse, hoping he had enough impulse control at the moment to comply.

23

Inside the building was a hallway with an elevator bank flanked by two glassed-in office suites.

One of the offices was dark and quiet; the other – the one closer to the blue dot of the location tracker – was illuminated. Frosted glass bore engraved lettering: Portland Field Project.

I looked at Jesse and pointed. He whispered to me: "That's weird."

"It's a hell of a lot more than weird," was all I could come up with.

I swung the door open and strode into a small office where a young man sat behind an IKEA sheet metal desk and stopped clicking away on his laptop to look up at us. Two BILLY bookcases displayed memorabilia from the erstwhile Portland Rockies and Portland Beavers baseball teams along one wall, while architectural renderings of an imagined future stadium on the Willamette filled the opposite one. Behind the man at the desk was another glass wall, frosted to the height of about seven feet, and containing a door.

"Can I help you gentlemen?" the man asked with a smile. He wore a lanyard with a clear plastic badge holder at the end, stuffed with cash and a Hop card. Lanyards and badge holders crossed – or perhaps merged – class boundaries in Portland. Identifiable on anyone from a homeless person to political senior staff, the lanyard meant you were part of the government-NGO blob. The lanyards represented rusted and porous buckets with which blob participants disinterestedly bailed water (or slurped it) from the sinking ship of state, calmly and steadily scooping as the level rose. Like a firearm on the hip of a border agent, the lanyard was not only functional but symbolic, a critical reminder of what one was dealing with.

I improvised.

"I had a meeting scheduled with… Hmm… It looks like there's already a meeting going on, though? Who's here today?"

It didn't work.

"I'm Justin and I can look you up and see what's on the schedule. Can I get your name and whom you were meeting with?" the young man asked.

I stalled for time, trying subtly to peer through the gap alongside the door to the conference room. "I was going to discuss a traffic and transit study related to parking."

"With whom, sir? And what did you say your name was?"

While I watched in surprise, Jesse pulled a metal cart – the "desk drawers" of the skeletal workplace – out from under Justin's desk and climbed up on it.

"He's with the building, needs to check the ceiling tiles," I lied.

None of it made a difference: as soon as Jesse got on the cart and looked through the upper, clear part of the conference room wall, he screamed, "It's him! It's Fernando!"

I strode to the door and yanked the handle. It didn't move – the door was locked. "I'm investigating a missing person," I declared, "and he's in there. Open this door."

Justin hesitated then cast his lot with the home team. "I'm sorry, that's Mark Marrenhous in there right now – Chuck's son? Marrenhous properties? – he's meeting with our board chair. You can't go in."

I pushed and kicked the thick glass door. Nothing.

"I'm going to have to call security," Justin said. He looked terrified by the whole situation but chose not to open the door. Instead, he got up and walked in the opposite direction, toward the office suite entrance, where he started dialing his phone.

I hit the door hard with my shoulder. It moved but didn't give. Drawing my 9mm, I stepped back and aimed toward the handle and lock. "Damn!" I said, realizing I wasn't about to fire toward the populated conference room. I aimed lower, thinking of shattering the glass closer to the floor. No good. A bad ricochet off steel floor plates and my next call with Altagracia might be the call I never wanted to make.

Before I could choose another course of action, I caught a shadow moving off to my left. I turned to see Jesse, with a fire extinguisher he'd retrieved from who-knows-where, lunging at the glass. He swung the extinguisher into the door and it cracked. Another swing and he had a hole in the thick tempered glass.

I crouched and looked through: it was Fernando, all right, along with four other men. A tall, beefy guy and a thinner one, both wearing dark suits, stood flanking Fernando, who was seated at a conference table. Next to him sat a man in a pale green dress shirt open at the collar – Marrenhous, I guessed – while, at the other end of the table, the fourth man sat wearing PNW fleece.

The men in suits pulled back the rolling chairs that Fernando and Marrenhous were sitting in, and placed themselves in front, protecting the men from anything coming from my direction.

"Open up!" I screamed and rammed the metal drawer cart into the broken glass. The opening was bigger now but still too small to enter.

In any case, I wasn't sure I wanted to enter, since I was looking through the hole at two chunky stainless steel automatics in the hands of the dark-suited men. Some sixth sense tingled – I saw a gold watch on the beefy man's wrist move in a significant way – and, before the thought fully registered, my unconscious mind dropped me flat to the floor.

That reflexive action helped me evade a barrage of gunfire that tore up the conference room door and wall.

I rolled to my right and caught a glimpse of Jesse, flat against the concrete and shielded from view by the BILLY bookcases. His eyes were wide and his face held shock, disbelief, and terror – this looked to be his first real gunfight and all he'd brought was internet gaming 'tude and a fire extinguisher. The particle-board BILLY wouldn't stop a bullet but the visual cover might be good enough if Jesse just stayed put.

I fired upward from my prone position, two rounds spraying shards of wood outward when they hit the conference table. By then, the bodyguards were tangled up tighter with Marrenhous, whose family name was on enough Portland buildings to make firing anywhere in his direction deeply unwise.

For a moment, it was unclear how the situation would evolve: I couldn't fight my way in to Fernando and the bodyguards weren't leaping to come out and bring their protectee toward my SIG.

Then the conference room turned into a giant opaque cloud of white.

Movement to my left again drew my attention: Jesse had dropped to the ground next to me, still holding the fire extinguisher, and he was blasting its contents into the conference room through a hole in the glass.

Things got quiet. Then I heard muted banging. The white cloud of extinguisher compound churned and slowly began to clear. After about thirty seconds, which felt like an hour, we could see into the conference room. No one was there. A door stood open at the rear of the room.

Knocking out more of the glass allowed me quickly to enter and cross to the open door: it led to a corridor, also empty, which terminated at a building exit. The whole crew was gone, including Fernando and the man in the fleece, who must have been the Field Project's chair. I stood and turned around to see Justin in the office suite doorway, phone still to his face. I holstered the SIG.

"You'd better stay put," he declared. "I'm on the phone with the cops."

I listened for a long moment and didn't hear a sound.

"Well why aren't you saying anything then?" I asked.

Sheepishly, he admitted he was still on hold and 911 hadn't taken his call yet.

I grabbed Jesse and muttered, "Walk. Just walk," in his ear as I pulled him toward the main entrance. Over my shoulder, I called out to Justin: "See, that's why we pay the high taxes here. Gets us clairvoyant BOEC operators who know you're an asshole and leave you on hold."

As soon as Jesse and I got out the door, we sprinted down the block toward the Miata. There was no one on the street to see us. My laptop was still under the floor mat. It was a near miracle – or maybe the gunfire had scared away would-be thieves. A moment of fumbling with the immobilizer and we were gone.

24

It was just past noon. We needed a chance to calm down and debrief so I led us to the food cart pod on Fifth. The armed guards near the gates looked bored. They patrolled quietly. Their necessity screamed. I carried the laptop with me as we filed past. We entered the fenced-in lot and immediately lined up for a pint of the strongest and bitterest West Coast IPA we could locate on a menu board.

"This place is actually pretty nice," Jesse commented, looking around the covered picnic area. "Those mobile bathrooms are super slick too – they have those same kind out by the bullpens at the ballpark in Yamhill. But the fence and the guards? Do all the food trucks have that now?"

The reality of what transpired hadn't sunk in for him yet, so I went along shooting the bull.

"Nah," I replied. "Mostly they don't have guards because mostly they don't have a big corporate sponsor. The magic is that, technically, this here is a private event. So they don't have to let the meth-heads swing machetes or burn the bathrooms. Whereas, in public," I raised my arm to gesture outside the beer garden, "menacing and arson are human rights."

"Now you're starting to sound like those guys online," Jesse said, as our beers appeared on the counter and we headed to a table. "So why do you stay in Portland? Not enough trouble to investigate anywhere else?"

"Hey…" I said. I almost told him not to be a wise-ass, but the kid had been shot at today and maybe thwarted serious bloodshed with his fire extinguisher stunt, even if everyone ended up gone and the kidnap count went up. "People put up with corruption and incompetence they really shouldn't, but their hearts are mostly in the right place."

He gave me a look like I had stumbled, drooling, off the short bus.

"Folks in Yamhill and elsewhere tolerate narrow-minded government-hating foolishness that they ought'n't to … but their hearts are also mostly in the right place."

Jesse gave a slightly sarcastic laugh. "Wouldn't want it on me to keep the peace, all I'm saying. Look at dad and Ashley. My bar's next in line to take a hit with these crooks. I dunno…"

"Just remember when you're getting revved up," I said, "The fight's a means to an end, not the end itself. And it's not a straight shot to a setup you can live with. No man gets violent asking for half of what he's owed. He fights for all of it even if he might come out with nothing. The picture in our heads, how we want it to be? That only comes from adding up all the fights, the losses and the wins. Like today…"

I felt like I had said too much already so I swallowed the rest.

"Not sure I totally get you. But I'll think about it. Really. But, today: what the hell happened?"

"I'm trying to put the thing together myself," I said. "One guy – the fleece at the end of the table – is head of the Field Project. He's taking a meeting with Mark Marrenhous. I hadn't ever seen Mark in person but I'd heard of him. He's Charles Marrenhous' son: heir to, and COO of, their real estate empire. That makes Mark the guy in the green shirt."

Jesse interjected, "I didn't know his name, but I've seen that dude before. He's been around the ballpark and with George Delany a bunch in Yamhill."

"Interesting. I wonder what the connection is. I also don't get why he had Fernando with him and brought the two goons. Either the goons were babysitting Fernando, who couldn't otherwise be convinced to go along, or else Marrenhous expected trouble at the meeting?"

"Or," Jesse suggested, "Marrenhous was bringing trouble *to* the meeting. I mean like he wanted to convince the Field Project guy of something in … a kind of a forceful way."

"Well, the Marrenhous family has been accused of brutal stuff over the years, but I was never sure how seriously to take the stories. Portland used to be shady as hell – I mean before the *Portlandia* days – and businesses around that long often have a … mixed history at some point. Or could be he's in the crosshairs like all the landlords now."

We had done some damage on our beers so I got up and ordered us another round and a cheesesteak for myself. I looked over and Jesse was picking up a slice of pizza from a different cart.

Back at the table, Jesse evinced a new excitement. "The tracker that was in my car when Fernando first ran into trouble, the one we followed," he began. "Like either he's got it with him or else someone who's messing with him has got it. Look on your laptop and see if it's got a location now."

I felt stupid. Or old. I chose to appreciate Jesse's energy. We took a look, but there was no position available.

"Would've been too much luck," I said.

We ate and drank for a while in silence.

Eventually, Jesse spoke up. "How do you plan to find Fernando now?"

"Aside from repeatedly checking to see if the tracker pops back up, I'm going to dig a little online and chat with a few people, get caught up on the latest Marrenhous conquests, misadventures and accusations. Make a list of locations they might accommodate someone who, uh, doesn't want to stay accommodated."

Jesse's phone buzzed. He left it face down on the table and didn't reflexively paw it like a cat after a mouse. I respected that.

"You mean the office buildings they own? Think they keep him locked up in one?"

"It's possible, although I'm thinking more like hotels or condos where they can brief the security and 'persuade' Fernando to stay put." I made the quotes with my fingers.

"I still don't get why they grabbed him in the first place."

"Yeah..." I said, trailing off and picking up my beer. In the pause, Jesse picked his phone up and took a look.

He softly said, "Shit," and began to stand up. "I better get back to Yamhill. Keep the bike locked up for me?"

"Sure. What's going on?"

"Lube shop where my dad works is done. They just told everyone they're closing at the end of the week. I hope they at least make payroll. Fuck. I don't know whether city problems are worse or..."

"The shop is local, right? In that town, you can bet they'll at least get their last check. But I'm sorry to hear it."

"Well, shit," Jesse said. "Gotta catch a break eventually, right?"

He turned and walked away pronouncing the rhetorical question. He waved a casual goodbye over his head as he exited past the guard and turned down the street toward his Miata.

Glancing at my watch, I planned out the couple of hours remaining until I was supposed to meet Isabelle.

25

I texted Manny, thinking I could borrow part of his security office at The Multnomah to do a little digging. He was looking for an excuse to get out, though, so he suggested meeting at a coffee shop in Old Town near Ankeny Square. He said he'd bring a laptop and we could double-team the problem.

The idea seemed reasonable and wouldn't take me far away, so I agreed and left the cart-pod-cum-*Biergarten*. Heavy clouds were blowing in from the east and the streets of Old Town were emptier than usual. I thought I sensed someone behind me a couple of times as I walked. I checked, expecting to see a vagrant, but saw no one at all.

A couple of blocks later I was sure I had a tail. I caught a fragmentary view here and there. Then I ducked into the entrance alcove of an empty building and tried to use the glass on the opposite side of the street to see who it might be.

Sure enough, someone advanced along the street then stopped not far from the alcove I was in. The reflection wasn't good enough to make out details but I was pretty confident it was the same person I'd spied tailing me. I was waiting and watching the street and the reflection when I heard a click and a creak behind me.

As I turned, my eyes widened. The door to the empty building was open. Flanking the inside of the doorway were the men in black coats and beanies who had appeared in my apartment two mornings prior. They reached toward me from opposite sides, grabbed my arms, and yanked me through the entrance.

When I caught my balance, I reached for my gun but my hand froze on the grip. The tall man had me covered – again – with his own weapon, from about five feet away. The short man half frisked me, gently pulled my hand away from the gun, then held my hands behind my back.

"Probably best if you keep your hands where he can see them," the short man said, gesturing with a nod toward his associate.

I stood there, waiting to see what was next. I looked around for a way out but kept my eye movements slow and gentle.

"Just a reminder to stick to your bread and butter and we'll be fine," said the guy holding my hands.

The tall man finally spoke. "What he's trying to say is: can the dinner date. You want to look for your pals from Yamhill? Go right ahead. But leave it at that."

The earth rumbled as a MAX train passed and the man momentarily looked outside, losing his focus on me. The gun drooped. I forcefully pulled my hands free from the shorter man and took a stride toward that gun.

"Maybe the two of you stay the hell – " I began, my hand closing on the slide of the man's automatic and steering it off to the side. His jacket flapped open with the movement of his arm and, inside the jacket, I caught a glimpse of a baseball logo on a leather case. Before the sense impression could resolve into information, I was hit with another 10,000 volts in the side. Or, as Manny had tried to explain it, a microcoulomb. Either way, I fell to the ground, the tall man clubbed me with the slide of his gun, and I blacked out.

When I regained awareness, I was lying in the doorway of that same building and someone was pulling at my shirt. At first I thought it was an unusually aggressive bum and I started flailing but, when my vision cleared, it was Manny trying to pull me to a sitting position. I whipped my head around, wondering if the guys in black were gone.

"Relax," Manny said. "The coast is clear for now. What happened?"

"I was being tailed and I ducked over here to take a look. I was facing the street when the door opened behind me. I got grabbed by the two guys who showed up in my apartment the other day. Did I tell you about that? Anyway, they gave me another warning and dialed up both the clarity of the language and the threat of force. They zapped me, Manny! That's twice in a week."

"Huh. Someone was tailing me on the way to the coffee shop as well. I'd swear it was a girl but I couldn't prove it. Anyway, I figured I'd let them follow if they wanted, then I saw your legs sticking out of the doorway here. Wasn't sure they were your legs at first; I walked over expecting to find an OD." He patted a fanny pack where he carried Narcan. "And here you are."

I'd only been out a couple of minutes. My laptop bag was still on the floor behind me. We walked around the corner to Java Rapids, which was empty that afternoon, ordered a couple of cortados, and sat at a massive slab of Oregon black walnut. The coffee had me mostly functioning again in minutes.

"There was something else. I'd swear I saw some kind of baseball wallet or badge holder inside the one guy's jacket."

"Baseball goons? That's a new one by me. I can look into it later at the hotel. What's the urgent on tap right now, though?" Manny asked with a squirrelish eagerness.

"Well, I need a crash course in the Marrenhous real estate empire, including nearby places suitable for accommodating a hostage and alleged history of zoning shenanigans. Maybe you can also help me rig up a monitor for a location tracker that's offline. Basically, ping me with a location as soon as one becomes available. And I've only got about two hours before the meeting I was just warned off of."

"I've got ninety minutes, but I think we can crank both of those with a little AI help. You make the robots do the research and I'll make them write your monitor script."

As a mostly solo practitioner, the advent of AI has been a godsend for my work. I let other people sweat the details on how good the latest models and services are. For me, the cheap alternative was usually nada; the expensive one I can't afford; and I'd find out fast enough if the AI's info is no good. It reminded me a bit of those factorization problems that are near impossible to solve but trivial to check. So I started a couple of research agents factoring the Marrenhous stuff for me.

Manny, it seemed, was a coding genius so long as he didn't have to do the coding. That is, he knew more than enough to tell the models what to code and he had decent instincts for doing a basic smoke test. Again, the alternative was zilch so we rolled the dice and got his AI-genned script running on a server somewhere. Not sure how or where, but the model told him how to do that part, too.

In a little while, I had a couple of reports to review. I double-checked the buildings the AI recommended and narrowed down the list. I also learned a couple of things about real estate and politics in Portland, mostly amounting to their being roughly coterminous until recently.

Then Manny and I sat around shooting the bull until he needed to get back to work. We buddied up for the walk to The Multnomah and I used a spare room to clean myself and brush off my outfit. When I looked almost passable, I headed a couple blocks away to attempt a rendezvous with a woman I'd never met but who was somehow connected to everything going on. Again, I got the sense I was being tailed but couldn't lock it down. When I got inside Big Pink, I was pretty sure I was both alone and also on about a dozen security cam feeds.

26

I walked down the building's ground floor internal arcade of closed up shops and lunch joints. They weren't entirely out of business yet, but with the last tenants leaving the skyscraper, it was a matter of time. I climbed stairs to the second floor, which provided a view down the lobby – still empty – and into large office suites – also empty – that had once commanded premium rents.

Further up, the third floor hosted a massive space, now entirely bare, spanning the pedestal and tower. Its locked door didn't vigorously resist. Mechanical elements yielded to classic picking tools and the electronic systems were offline, probably to make things easy for a leasing rep if by some miracle a tenant showed interest. Inside the tower segment of the suite, a door near the main elevator bay was unlocked and led to a service lift. I rode to thirty where Portland City Grill was located, once a nationally top-grossing restaurant. The Grill drew enough tourists to keep the lights on, supplemented by a handful of awkward first-daters and a handful of older power players wallowing in nostalgia.

I slowly found my way from the service corridor to the front of the house, where the space was cool, dark, and empty. The sky was still fairly bright at that hour, but a sort of special coating on the skyscraper's glass gave the impression of tinted sunglasses and produced an early dusk. Big

Pink had integral 80s-style shades, a middle-aged man holding fast to youth.

Making my way around the enormous dining room toward the bar, I caught sight of what was unmistakably Isabelle Delany. I'd like to say I recognized her from some society photo, but it was more process of elimination: she was the only woman in the joint. As I approached, two men in nondescript business casual scurried away from her toward the elevators. It might have been useful to follow them or, if I had a partner, send a tail that way. But, flying solo, I had to clear my mind and focus on making a decent impression.

Isabelle leaned against the bar; she intimidated despite the casual posture. For one thing, she was tall even without heels. For another, she had on an evening gown in off-white satin the likes of which rarely appeared anywhere in Portland aside from a screen. Her soft, girlish face, pink lips and dark eyes conjured a feeling of innocence; golden blonde hair in a classic bob with slightly wavy layers added a counterpoint of elegant sophistication.

"So this is how farm girls clean up when they're coming to the city?" I asked, coarse humor being the only possible open for a guy like me addressing a girl like her.

Against the marble bar in the dim light and dressed as she was, she looked so much like a character from a 20th-century film that I half-expected Mid-Atlantic accent and diction. That's not what came out.

"I figured why not have a little fun with – well, never mind, maybe we'll get to that. I'm sorry, I know it's kinda silly. Just pretend I'm wearing jeans like a normal person… Jack? Jack Louis, right?"

Oregon country speech punctuated with a relaxed grin made something liquify deep inside me. This day just kept going.

"That's me. And, actually, mind if we get a drink before…" I looked around the entire dining room. It was empty, but when I turned back, a man had materialized behind the bar. "Before we get down to it?"

"I could use one myself. My car got blown up this morning. Firebombed. But I bet you already knew that."

A look toward the barman got his attention. I ordered a martini, olives, with a Willamette Valley gin – a double – and paused for Isabelle. She asked for the same.

"You look pretty good for someone who was almost blown up," I said.

"I was thirty feet away when it went off and a small tree blocked a bunch of … stuff … that flew in my direction. I was either really lucky and whoever it was screwed up, or they were sending a very emphatic warning."

"I can buy that analysis. Either way, any idea who might have been behind it?"

"I'm not sure, but I think it has something to do with the stadium land deal that part of my family has been working on," she said. "I better rewind. George – you know George, right? I saw you with him at the party after the Pioneers game in Yamhill. He's my cousin. He and his dad – my uncle – well they're gonna be out of the minor league ball business if a big league team comes to Portland. They've got some money, they love the game, and George, he just loves being the man around town. So they wanted to get involved in the Portland stadium development on the river here."

She paused and I half interrupted. "OK, before we get to the car bombing part, lemme make sure I'm caught up with you." I looked around the cavernous space, which was still vacant save for the barman who set our drinks onto cocktail napkins. I lowered my voice a bit anyway. "This development thing: this is a deal where George gets some special zoning rights or something, super valuable even if there's no team, but it's a tricky sell at city hall?"

Isabelle looked sad and shocked. "Oh, no. Nothing like that. No. Although I've heard him talking about something bigger and ... er ... less straightforward. Something like what you were saying. That's this other group of owners, not George. A man named Marrenhous. I'll bet it's his thugs who blew up my car."

"And why would they do something like that? Aren't they part of this same deal with your family?" I tried again.

"Definitely not. I know they're trying something sketchy and George would never do that. See, George is the biggest owner of the team. The Marrenhous family, they're part of a company that owns a smaller piece, a company called Summer Fun. I know: funny name for the business, right? But, anyway, they need my cousin to go along with it, to sign on, or ... or ... or else they need him to back away so they can proceed. Something like that."

"OK, I'm gonna sip my drink here for a minute and think about this," I told her. And that's what I did. Was she confused? Lying? Honest, but wrong? Something felt genuine in a way I couldn't articulate, and yet the facts as I had them didn't lean in her direction.

I decided to go with the straight dope. "Look, Ms. ... Delany. Your car was blown up. That I know. I saw it myself. And you're charming as hell. You got the glamorous mystery meetup here working for you. On top of that, I like your family and I like your little town. But here's the thing: a witness – Jesse Owens – saw George with Mike Marrenhous many times over the course of months in Yamhill. At a recent meeting, the guy named Bunton who runs Summer Fun LLC – the company you just said Marrenhous was part of – he was in Yamhill at the bar next to the ballpark, working on a land development deal and George's name was all over the documents."

"I'm sure that ... No!" she said emphatically. "Let's see those documents. I'm sure I can explain it."

"Unfortunately, I don't have them," I admitted. I decided not to mention that the woman who got the closest look at them had been run off the road shortly thereafter and then locked with me in a freezer where we were both left for dead.

"Jesse... Jesse probably saw them together just on team business. You know Jesse's also my cousin. Well, sort of. Peggy's my first cousin, which makes Jesse ... my cousin once removed I think. He's been around the team so much he's seen everyone together."

"You and Jesse ... Peggy ... OK, I guess practically everyone is related in Yamhill County," I said with a little snark.

"Stop it," Isabelle said. She looked like she really was hurt.

My phone buzzed with a message from Abby.

"I'm sorry," I said to Isabelle. "I need to make a quick call. Can we continue this in a couple of minutes?"

"I needed to visit the ladies' anyway," she replied, pivoting from the bar and turning, her back to me as she walked away. The rear silhouette in that gown was a sight. I watched until it disappeared around a corner and then I picked up my phone, walked to a distant part of the restaurant, stood looking at Mt. Hood out the window, and dialed.

27

Abby picked up and got right into it. "How friendly are you with the cops?"

"We get on pretty well. Occasionally step on each other's feet, but in this town it's an 'enemy of my enemy is my friend' kinda situation…"

"Any chance you could talk them into letting me go?"

"It generally doesn't work that way. If you've been arrested, I can't help you, but the revolving door will spit you back onto the street in a few hours … unless you've killed someone."

"They say I'm not officially under arrest as long as I hang out here and answer questions. I … was pushing my luck around the South Waterfront. They say I was interfering with the crime scene where the car got blown up and that they could arrest me for criminal trespass. But I swear I was a hundred yards away when they caught up to me. Anyway, I sat here in the station for two hours, then a detective … this Detective Whidby … shows up and is asking me a bunch of stuff I don't know anything about. But no, they haven't arrested me, just, kinda persuaded me to stay here. But I'm done now."

Frickin' Whidby, I thought to myself, laughing. "It's your lucky day, kid," I told Abby. "I know the detective. Lemme talk to him." Brendan Whidby and I went way back.

She put him on the phone.

"Hey Witless – Jack Louis."

"Jesus Christ, Jack, you're mixed up with this somehow?"

"Hey, I was just trying to find a missing kid ... well, minor league pitcher ... after his mom called me. But things have ... metastasized."

"Yeah? Well, be careful. There seem to be a lot of players – huh no pun intended – here and I'm not sure I know all of 'em. There are feds sniffing around. There's a couple of guys here from – get this – Major League Baseball has its own Pinkertons or something. Mostly ex-cops of different flavors poking around to keep the league's nose clean. A couple of 'em found your friend here sitting in the back seat of their car. Which was parked near the bombing. Asked us to, uh, invite her in for a conversation. You know her how?"

"OK, I don't know her well. But aside from being annoying in the way that journalists usually are and freelance-blogger-type journalists always are ... I think she's OK. Lemme put it this way: she's been on the receiving end of some shit and, as far as I can tell, she just likes to snoop and write about it. She's assigned herself to the Willamette River beat. I don't know what she knows. Hey. These private baseball cops: what do they look like?"

Detective Whidby obliged with a description. "White guys, middle-aged, one tall with a mustache, one short, black coats and beanies. Pale. Dark jeans, cop shoes."

"Ah, shit. OK, I've got a wild story for you. That and a beer soon if you think you're ready to let Abby go?"

"Sure thing. I've got real work to do."

I signed off and returned to the bar. Isabelle was there fidgeting with a credit card slip.

"I have to go for now," she said. "But I got your drink and all I ask in return is you give me another chance to explain about George. I'll be at the Ritz."

I thought for a minute.

"This is gonna be a downgrade in accommodations. Hoo boy. But since someone's at least pretending to try and kill you, maybe a more secure location would make sense. If you can stomach it, head over to The Multnomah. It's right – " I turned and pointed out the window " – down there. At the desk, ask for Manny Gil. I'll make sure he knows you're coming. Tell him to bring you by the bar there at some point too. No view like this here, but they make a hell of a martini."

"Well," she said, clearly conflicted and trying to recalibrate the attitude it took to go anywhere – let alone in Portland – in that gown, "I'll consider it."

She headed toward the elevators, paused for a moment, and half turned. For just the briefest of moments she delivered a knowing smirk, then vanished around the corner.

I wandered back to the window and looked out, vertical down to the ground. Portland was lately in the news for an outbreak of dysentery on the streets, but from thirty floors up you'd never know it – even if the windows weren't sealed shut. In the building's heyday, the Grill was a place to take in a view from the mountains and rivers to Forest Park and to make plans which utterly neglected the down and out. Today, Portland's most iconic skyscraper – "US Bancorp Tower" officially – was empty, on the market for pennies, and a different crowd held the gavels at city hall and at the courthouse. Any chance for a middle way had blown by fast.

I thought about Jesse's frustration. Often, there was no use fantasizing about compromise. Complex systems don't course correct, not really. When they look stable, they're playing you for the fool, showing you attractors that generate quasi equilibria where there are none. Big words, but I'd learned this not in some university lecture but the hard way, getting kicked around in the insurance biz.

Law of averages, I used to say, claiming troubled neighborhoods would stabilize, shape up. But that's not how it worked. Fraud and crime hit a certain level and then some latent Schelling model had its way with me and with everybody else: we'd clean up outstanding cases, bail out, and never write a policy there again. The neighborhoods filled with burnt-out shells of buildings and stayed like that for a generation.

Then again, if you averaged growth over the centuries, the curve almost looked smooth.

28

A rattle of glassware behind me said the bartender was prepping for happy hour and dinner. My watch had 4:40 p.m. I thought about driving to Yamhill and getting a deeper look into into George's projects. I could stay at my trailer, work that night, and be ready to go the next morning. But I also had this list, courtesy of the AI, of Marrenhous properties. Some I knew well and some were only planned. About five, though, appeared built but not yet operational. Those places were great candidates for stashing Fernando. With some sweat and risk, I could try and get a closer look. Or I could talk to Hannah in Permitting and Development, find out enough to rank the buildings, and maybe even pick up some intel that would help me get inside.

I really wanted to catch Hannah at the office. After all, this was official, public info – mostly – that I was after. I could grab the next bus and hop off a block from Hannah near PSU.

It was 4:54 p.m. when she saw my text and led me back past a gaggle of disgruntled permit-seekers hoping for news on the city's latest demands before they lost another day of work. My request was no challenge for her and, within a minute, she had my list filtered, sorted and printed out. Four of the buildings had utilities live and were ready to go, save final inspections. Of those, location and degree of private access recommended a particular order for the search. I thanked Hannah profusely and prepared to leave when she grabbed my arm.

Leaning in, she whispered, "You should get him out of town ASAP and ... here ... hang on."

She straightened up, sorted a couple of items on her desk, grabbed her jacket and, in a loud voice intended for the benefit of coworkers and any remaining petitioners, declared, "It's five o'clock. Time to go get that drink we were talking about."

I played along and followed her out. When I started to ask what was up, she signaled to wait, and led me about a block to an off-campus institution with cheap drinks and a quiet, empty lounge. The pub's owner had been cancelled a year or two prior for counting four fingers when a mob wanted her to see five, with the result that business was slow until students arrived later at night. Student allegiance to alcohol and low prices apparently exceeded loyalty to groupthink, and America kept rolling forward.

In a dark rear corner booth, I drank coffee while Hannah slammed an IPA. "The feds are here sniffing around and it would be smoothest for Fernando if he were gone," she said.

"I'm getting better at taking the not-so-subtle hints," I replied. "So the feds are into this tangle of baseball and zoning corruption? Can you give me anything else? I'll buy you and your girlfriend dinner. And wine." I regretted the words as soon as they left my mouth. My client was broke, so that dinner would hurt when it came out of my pocket.

My regret lessened when, after fifteen seconds of silence, Hannah opened up. "Not quite. If the feds got involved in every crooked local land deal, the whole country would shut down. And after the drug stuff, the player smuggling, the Braves, gambling... The feds are taking a break from baseball. MLB has to keep its own house clean for now and they know they might lose their antitrust exemption if they don't."

"Well what the hell else is there then?" I asked, confused.

"It starts with racketeering at the county," she said in a half-whisper. "There's hundreds of millions of federal dollars being diverted into the hands of a few dozen people in a kind of pyramid scheme of patronage. It's smaller than the New York crime families, but Portland has a lot of enemies in D.C. and not a lot of friends. I don't know who the linchpin targets are; I only know the guy they're looking for most of all. His alias is Oscar. Like in any bureaucracy, low-level players sometimes get ambitious and do stupid things. In this case, Oscar's lackeys started shaking down your boy Fernando."

"For what? I'm pretty sure a Dominican minor league pitcher hasn't got any dough and no one cares if he – what? – throws a small-town game?"

"It's the dumbest shit in the world. Oscar found out Fernando gets paid to courier interesting documents. And Oscar wants to tap a vein and collect money from the baseball development deal because he's part of MultCo and it's crooks all the way down, so of course he does. Well, Fernando is on a H2-B visa like most minor leaguers. He can't work outside of baseball. ICE doesn't give a shit, but Fernando doesn't know that. And if anyone thinks Fernando's mixed up with Oscar, he'll end up in a much worse place than deported. Easiest thing: get him out of town and fast."

"I'm grateful for the tip, but I still don't know where he is. If I can figure out the mechanics and the bad mojo in the development deal, I'll be farther along."

"Amy said you've got balls and brains, and I've seen a hint of both, so … if you want to help yourself, your client, and Uncle Sam all in one go, Chuck Marrenhous' boat is currently tied up at the marina near where we first met. It is believed that Oscar will be showing up for a little boat ride to attempt some negotiations in about an hour. If you can figure out how to get onboard and stow away…"

It was dicey as hell but irresistible.

"Just one question," I began. "Why aren't feds doing the sneaking?"

"They just might. But for now the paperwork is tangled up with a couple of judges. Long story. If it clears in time, you might get company. I'll send them your info so at least they know to point the boom sticks in another direction, if possible."

"And you'll send me their info too?"

"I don't think so, cowboy. And seriously, try not to do anything crazy. The Marrenhous goons are experienced and Oscar is, uh, rumored to have access to a guard armory. So they've got more hardware than you. Plus it's twenty years per count if they get caught, so they have more motivation too."

"Thanks. Really. And I'm motivated. Just by different things," I said.

Our drinks were empty and I had a long night ahead of me, so we walked outside. I went to shake hands at the door but was surprised by a hug. Maybe things were going to get worse. Or maybe she was just a hugger.

29

I took TriMet back to my apartment to prepare for the stowaway-stakeout operation. I donned a dive-skin-type full-length suit in case I ended up in the water and added a swim vest that could hold things for quick access: phone, gun, extra magazine, flashlight, and Leatherman. Then I pulled hiking shorts and a flannel over all that so I'd look like less of a freak. In the Pacific Northwest, anyway, I'd look like less of a freak. I grabbed a corded sports bag and inserted a dry bag inside with binoculars, emergency gear and miscellaneous supplies. Last, I traded leather for neoprene aqua shoes. I said a silent prayer to Chinese sporting goods manufacturing, despite the troubling implication for Oregon's own outdoor gear industry.

Another twenty minutes got me back to the marina where I milled around with a sparse tourist crowd on the promenade and scoped out Chuck Marrenhous' boat, a roughly fifty-foot yacht humorously named the *Anchor Tenant*. The only visible action was a single black-clad and bored-looking man, a steward-cum-security-officer, pacing the deck. Occasionally, a van would pull up in the circle at the bottom of Montgomery and a man would wheel a dolly along the gangway and onto the boat. Binoculars revealed festive plans: a rich variety of food, wine, booze, even an ice sculpture rolled aboard.

A while later, the vans were gone and a limo appeared. While the new arrivals got the glad handing and the boat show-off tour for first timers, I clambered down and headed for another craft two slips beyond the *Tenant*. I climbed up, nonchalantly pretended I was doing a little cleaning, then moved to the next boat. Another careful scan of the Marrenhous craft suggested the "welcome aboard" tour was elsewhere so I flopped over, grabbed the bow rail, and scrambled up.

I had access to an oversized anchor locker and hopped in. I wouldn't be able to hear or see anything, but I could hide out and look for a better spot once we were underway. Another few minutes brought the noise and vibration of rumbling engines and we slowly began moving downstream. Cell tower triangulation gave my phone a decent guess at our position and motion on the river.

After ten minutes, I hoped everyone had settled in to eat, drink, and discuss. Popping the hatch a crack revealed no one nearby. I climbed onto the foredeck, remaining on hands and knees.

Moving along the deck, I could see – through portholes – the conclave taking place. Chuck Marrenhous I recognized from his numerous appearances in civic, society, and press events over the years. His security man looked the part with an earpiece and the rest. There were three additional men whom I didn't recognize. One looked like a wannabe Blackwater mercenary, sporting over-the-top gear. One had the Mike Vining look, like he'll garrote you and you'll spend your last breath wondering why the accountant in the dorky glasses chose violence. And one was a young guy, maybe late twenties, red hair and pale freckled skin in a white pressed shirt and black slacks. I guessed this was Oscar or, at least, Oscar's representative. The whole gang were seated in a leather sectional watching the Blazers game on a TV mounted opposite. The civilian participants were drinking something dark from short, heavy rocks glasses – I guessed Old Fashioned, Negroni, or straight whiskey. It seemed business was not yet underway and I wanted to wire audio before it began. We were already past the St. Johns Bridge, nearing the container terminals, destination unclear.

I crawled further along the deck, turned a corner and had direct line of sight to the meeting. But the noise of the engines, water, and wind were still too loud to hear conversation. I improvised a wireless listening device with an earbud, waited for an attention grabbing moment in the basketball game, and flipped the 'bud down onto the floor where it skittered under the legs of the group and came to rest just about perfectly beneath the front edge of the sectional.

A few taps later and I could hear everything through the other earbud: the game, the "nice boat" chit-chat, even the clinking of glasses on the table. I shuffled backward, farther away, and hunkered down to wait.

After about five minutes, the red-haired kid started fidgeting then spoke up assertively.

"Mr. Marrenhous. I'm so glad we were able to get this meeting set up. Thanks again for hosting here. It's amazing. I think we just have a few tiny things to sort out and … everything is going to go super smoothly with your new projects."

Suddenly, Chuck appeared less at ease than he had a moment prior.

"A few tiny things," he repeated. His eyes were still on the game. He poured more into his glass. "Super smoothly, eh? Is that a promise?"

"I'm pretty confident…" the younger man began. Marrenhous cut him off. Some energy or anger was rising in his tone.

"Robert. Robert O'Shea. They call you Robbie, right? Can I call you Robbie?"

There was a pause but no reply.

"Robbie, how are the folks? They're down in Canyonville – that's where you're from, isn't that right?"

"Yes. They're OK. I don't see them too much."

"Because you came all the way up here. To Portland. Not a popular choice in Douglas County. You did it to get ahead, though, right? Canyonville is poorer than the worst neighborhoods in Portland."

"Well, yes, there is a lot more opportunity here."

"Like the one you came to negotiate today."

"I just meant…"

"Look, son, I know exactly what you meant. There's a deep, wide trough here to feed from for you and your friends. There's nothing coming your way – or your folks' way – in Canyonville. We're just leaving them to die down there, I guess. So, Robbie, you know who I am, and now you know I know who you are. But I need to find out: what's your part in all of this? What do you get exactly?"

"I'm just doing my job at the county, Mr. Marrenhous."

The elder Marrenhous looked displeased. "Let's watch a bit more of the game, son," he said, turning away and looking intently at the television.

My phone said we were coming up past Kelly Point Park and maneuvering into the Columbia River.

A bit later, halftime began on the TV and Marrenhous turned back to O'Shea.

"You were going to tell me your cut in all this?"

"I'm just here doing a job," he started to say. Marrenhous gave the tiniest twitch of his eye in the direction of his security man, who immediately backhanded the kid across the mouth so hard he nearly fell off the couch.

The kid tried to regain his composure, noticed the stream of blood dripping from his mouth onto the bright white shirt, and became agitated, looking around wildly.

"Calm down," Chuck said. "Sorry about all that, but I'm trying to have a conversation here and I'm not sure whether you're ready to have it. Now, what is your cut?"

"Um… $900K over three years."

"That's it? Nobody wants to share with you?"

"No one is sharing anything. The 900 is taxpayer money. I just pay myself grants through an org and everyone OK's it."

"In addition to your county job."

"I, uh, don't see why not."

"OK, see, now we're getting somewhere. So that's your personal stake. Me, I'd've asked for more, but then again I run actual businesses, so it's a bit different. Now what exactly does your gang want?"

"Eight percent, with a minimum of $25 million."

"The taxes here are brutal," Chuck laughed.

"So we're good with that?" asked O'Shea.

"I heard what you said, now I'm going to think about it."

They watched the game for another five minutes or so. Then Chuck stood up and waved for the kid to get up. "Before we go further, I want to show you something. I need you to understand a bit of context."

They climbed up toward the deck of the boat on the side opposite where I was crouching. The sun was setting and the breeze on the river picking up. I ascended a ladder to the bridge deck and pulled myself on my belly across to the port side. I lay barely four feet above their heads.

Across the water were the lights of Vancouver, Washington's waterfront development. Chuck stretched his arm out and began talking to Robbie.

"See that? It's pretty nice, isn't it? Families out walking. Lights. Restaurants. Playgrounds. Clean bathrooms. That whole thing should be in Portland. Have you been over there? Take a good look. No fucking fentanyl zombies, no parents pulling their kids away from needles and foil and piles of human shit everywhere. No tents. No anarchists lighting the place up and handing out junk for bums to strew around later.

"My family has been building Portland for five generations and I wanted to build something like that. I'd still like to do it, down by the ballpark. But that can't happen, now, can it? In Portland, your goddamned crew has destroyed my family's properties and the city along with them. Why? I don't even know. Pandering to a bunch of toddlers who scream and smash shit and light the place on fire when they're in a bad mood? What the fuck kind of leadership is that? It's the kind that lets you and your buddies pocket all the money that was supposed to clean things up, was supposed to help the addicts, house the people in the tents.

"And now," he growled, grabbing Robbie's upper arm and yanking him nearly over the gunwale, "they have the balls to send you to try and shake me down for $25 million? Lemme tell you something, kid. You won't shake my family down and your commie groupies won't shake us off this city, either. Fifty years from now, we'll still be here. If there are any jobs for your kids, they'll be cleaning my sewers. I'll bring in a goddamned paramilitary to hang on to this town if that's what it takes. You ought to fuckin' know better. You're from Canyonville."

He fell silent for a bit, still looking across at the lively, floodlit Vancouver waterfront.

"Now, I'm not entirely unwilling to compromise. I'll give you something. Not $25 mil, but something. And this," he gestured to indicate the Vancouver promenade again, "this you motherfuckers owe me. It's a kind of debt and it's collecting interest."

"Hey, Stevie!" Marrenhous called out to the mercenary-looking character leaning over the side.

"Stevie, give Mr. O'Shea here the rest of the tour. Robbie, you be extra careful. Even on a nice safe boat like this, accidents happen."

Blackwater grabbed Robbie and dragged him astern while Chuck descended into the lounge. I tried to scramble around to see what was happening with O'Shea, but it was too dark.

A shrieking scream pierced the night, followed by a sequence of obscenities, another scream, and then silence.

Sixty seconds later, I heard footsteps. Blackwater was back and settled into the lounge with everyone else … except Robbie.

I debated my next steps. I could hide out – it appeared we were now on our way back to Portland. I could look around for Robbie. Getting into it with Marrenhous and his guys seemed off the table. This is a boat full of assholes, I thought. And maybe I'm one of 'em.

Robbie was crooked and stupid and too young to be doing what he was doing if he wanted to live to see Chuck's age. On the other hand, the kid probably didn't know what he was signing up for when, in desperation, he moved to a place with triple the median income of his hometown and took a job in its only growth industry: machine politics.

Chuck was a famous ballbreaker and patriarch of a family that owned nine figures in real estate, or maybe just a bit shy with the current state of the market. He ought to be a bit more gracious and someone should tell him it isn't the 1980s anymore. That said, his family had donated six parks, built two museums and a couple of hospital buildings, sponsored every civic event, and bailed out the library one time when the county lost its funding in a shady deal with shady pals. Maybe the folks running the city and county owed him a break.

I wasn't sure what the hell these people deserved, but luckily that wasn't my problem. My job was trying to figure out how to keep bad things from getting worse. Or at least make 'em get worse slower than they otherwise would.

30

Robbie had been gone a long time. Something was up, so I started looking for him. It was a small boat – couldn't be that hard, right?

Drunken chatter suggested the exciting part of the night was over. I exploited the darkness and began systematically prowling the craft.

I had covered nearly all of the exposed, accessible areas and was approaching the stern on the main deck, port side, when I stepped in something sticky. I crouched and turned my light on to discover blood and a decent amount of it. Broad ribbons connected the pool by my foot to another, nearer the gunwale. In the other direction, a thin stream led to a hatch. I turned the light back off and regretted – yet again – being too poor or, perhaps, too cheap to get decent night goggles. I silently swore to gift myself at least a monocular if the hatch didn't lead to a fatal ambush. With 9mm drawn, I grabbed the latch handle and threw the cover open.

There was no light inside and nothing attacked me, but I did see movement. I leaned forward and heard a shuffling noise. The boat turned and a shaft of moonlight illuminated a bloody figure huddled against the opposite corner of a storage locker: Robbie O'Shea.

"Don't kill me," he said in a hoarse, scratchy voice that just surpassed the engine, wind, and river noise.

"I'm not here to kill anybody," I said. I turned my light on again and pointed it at Robbie. There was a lot of blood but he was moving around OK. "What the hell happened here?"

"The commando guy, he... he... he tried to kill me."

"Tried" seemed unlikely. Commando guy could have broken Robbie in half and thrown him overboard with one arm. If Robbie was alive, there had been no earnest attempt at murder.

"Come 'ere," I said. "Lemme see what happened to you." I pulled a small first aid kit out of my bag along with some wipes in a Ziploc. Someone had smashed this kid's nose and done a bit of additional damage high on the side of his forehead. Both injuries meant a ton of blood but weren't exactly life threatening.

"Who the hell are you?" he asked.

"Name's Louis. I'm a neutral party. Been collecting some info tonight for a friend and trying to stay out of trouble. So this guy, he took you behind the woodshed?"

"Huh?"

He didn't understand the expression.

"Brought you out here to smack you around a bit, help make his boss' point about the money?"

As the adrenaline abated, the kid's face sagged along with the strength of his assertion: "Not exactly. It's my own damned fault. He just yelled at me a bunch. He did hold me over the side like he was gonna push me into the river, but he didn't do it. I... uh..."

He held up an empty military-style holster.

"I pulled a gun on him. It wasn't even loaded. My boss gave it to me. An M17 they got from the Oregon Guard. Look, this isn't loaded either."

He pulled a mag out of a pouch and held it up – empty.

"I pointed the gun at him and he didn't even flinch, just smashed me in the nose. Then he took the gun away, hit me in the head with it…" He felt the spot where a deep cut was still bleeding. "I think the sight caught me right here. Then he threw it in the river and put me in this locker."

"You're lucky you're not dead," I said, wiping the wound down. I put some gauze and tape on his head. The nose had stopped bleeding but would need professional attention if Robbie didn't want to look like a boxer. "Keep pressure on this and have a doc look at the nose when you get back to shore. While I'm giving free advice, do some serious thinking about your career path."

"Uh. Yeah, OK."

I still had my earbud in and the cabin had gone silent. A moment later, I heard what sounded like Chuck Marrenhous taking a phone call. It wasn't on speaker – I only heard his side of the conversation. Some nonspecific talk about plans began. I wanted to take a look but paused momentarily to glance back at Robbie.

"The boss who gave you the SIG … wanna tell me who that was?"

"They'll kill me if I name names, but if you heard the conversation before… Well, the county only has five commissioners, so you do the math."

I turned and walked toward the cabin, leaving O'Shea in his own mess in the storage locker.

31

Once again, I set up on the bridge deck just above one of the entryways to the lounge. I could see and hear Chuck. I got dates, I got a lot of "Almost done? It should have been done last fucking week!" But no specifics until he began his peroration:

"So you're telling me after all of this, you've gotten nowhere with George? He thinks he's going to build in Portland and follow all the rules, this standup guy, everyone's trusty buddy, like he's still down in that goddamned dusty town? I don't care if the Yamhill yokels think he's a hero. See if he can buy a damned little league team on his own. Motherfucking George Delany. See if he can get permits for a damned food truck near the ballpark without my help. So he's sponsoring scholarships and he's leading the July Fourth Parade and paying off dental bills for the migrants' kids? No one fucking cares! If you're completely sure he won't get on board, then tell him: he either signs the waivers and gets out of the way or I'll negotiate with that sonofabitch's next of kin!"

He went silent for a bit then spoke a final, quiet line: "Yes, only if you have to. But yes."

Two things went through my mind as we sailed past downtown, slowed, and approached the marina. It seemed I owed Isabelle an apology. And I had to get the hell off this boat.

I lowered myself over the side and, when we were just a dozen yards or so from the docks, I dropped into the water and swam through the brutal cold toward the Tom McCall Bowl beach. Sixty seconds later, I walked out of the water. I startled some teenagers who were giggling, sharing a blunt and a six pack off to my right. On my left, a fent-bent mope didn't notice me at all. After swapping my wet top for a dry T-shirt, I double-timed it toward The Multnomah to see Isabelle.

32

A text from Manny told me Isabelle was in the "secure wing." The wing was a joke we shared, referring to a cluster of adjoining rooms on the northeast corner of the seventh floor. The wing suffered perennially malfunctioning climate control, power, and water. Blocked from availability for general guests, the rooms served us on occasion as a sort of hideout or safe house and I headed straight there.

In the elevator, I wondered if my HMO's mobile app could find me a lepidopterist for a listen at my stomach. Maybe it was hunger and not the strange state I feared Isabelle would evoke in me. As I approached the hallway corner, I observed a room door partly open, resting on the security latch, lights on within. The butterflies vanished, replaced by more tractable and familiar tension. None of the doors should have been open if a car bombing target wanted a peaceful night's sleep.

Stealthily, I approached the door, squinted at the opening and listened to the sounds of silence. I drew the SIG, spun and slammed the door open. My eyes swept the room, meeting nothing and no one. Inside, a cursory check confirmed the room was empty. Something was wrong. Even more wrong, I felt an unexpected and unwelcome emotional reaction that distracted from calculating the next necessary action. A flash of heat lit up my forehead and my brain went blank. I threw some cold water on my face and dialed Manny.

"Hey. We've got a problem," I declared. Precisely the kind of useless statement I was trained not to make in a challenging situation.

"Well," Manny replied, "we frequently have a lot of problems. What's on your mind tonight?"

"Isabelle. She's not here. The room was open," I stammered.

"Ah, yeah. Sorry. She's here. Not there exactly. She wanted to shower and there's no hot water in the secure wing this week. The most secure spot with working plumbing is the Presidential Suite up top. Hasn't been booked all year and it's due for a cleaning so they let me put her in there. Separate elevator, special windows, no one will mess with her."

I was embarrassed, flummoxed, and then further embarrassed at the former two facts.

"Oh."

"Sorry, I should've sent an update."

I needed to act my age. "Not at all, it's just been a long day. Meet me downstairs and lemme grab a card to get up?"

A few minutes later, elevator doors opened on an antechamber of the Presidential Suite with a secondary door to the main living space. I knocked and called out.

The door swung open on Isabelle in a hotel robe and slippers, with the same playfully angry smile I'd left a lifetime ago in the City Grill bar.

"This is a pretty nice room. I've never been up here before." Figured I'd start slow. "Is everything … OK?"

"Can't complain about the accommodations," she said, gesturing at a Louis XV-style sofa in velvet brocade and then over to the windows. "Hell of a view in the daytime. Across the river, the leaves are all orange and gold. Mt. Hood right in your face. A girl could get used to this."

I knew the view she was talking about. In between the river and the mountains, a foreshortening effect from the shallow angle created an illusion of continuous forest. Sparsely planted expanses of Portland's east side vanished into a sylvan landscape from a long ago time.

"You know there's no restaurant in the hotel?" she asked.

I did, in fact, know that. There had been a damned good one just a week prior. The owner had recently cried on my figurative shoulder and given me a souvenir mug. I didn't bring it up.

"Manny got me some coffee – he's a sweetie. But I'm starving. Let's go find some food – you can be my bodyguard, right? Maybe I'll forgive you for insulting my cousin. You can act like a professional and try looking for the real bad guy instead of throwing accusations around."

Testosterone screamed yes but I softly reminded her that we were up against car bombs and worse. I told her I'd pick something up, asked what she'd like, and she said, "Surprise me."

I headed to the street where I experienced the quintessential Portland paradox: I had to step over bodies and excrement less than fifty yards from a Moroccan food truck with cuisine so famous that Eurotrash influensters 'grammed it on the daily next to their fake private jet bubbly shots. While the truck's operator was pulling together a few things one wasn't likely to find in Yamhill or Newberg – a veggie and a lamb tagine, rfissa, couscous and khobz – I ducked into a convenience store and added some West Coast to my North Africa with a triple IPA for myself and something less vicious for Isabelle. On the way back to the hotel, I grabbed a Voodoo Doll for dessert – a can't-lose no matter the situation.

When I got upstairs and laid out the haul on the suite's china, we ate ravenously for a few minutes. She wasn't ready to stop, but I took a breather to pronounce the apology I'd been rehearsing ever since Marrenhous cursed Delany on the boat. In my mind's eye, there had been some groveling, but in the real world I kept it on the level.

"I appreciate your saying that," Isabelle replied between bites. "And yeah, I can see how – without investing in character study of George – it might not be obvious that he'd buck the Oregon tradition of scamming taxpayers and laying claim to any resources one can get one's hands on." She paused for a bit. "Anyway, I hope you can see we're all on the same side here."

"I get it. And, honestly, after the times I spent at that ballpark, the thought of George… Well, all kinds of people do horrific things every day. And I see more than my fair share of it. Still, it does feel nice when the worst isn't true."

I felt myself losing focus. It had been one of the longer days I'd experienced, particularly since my age got a four at the front of it. The triple IPA wasn't helping either. But the spandex – I was still wearing the absurd dive suit – was uncomfortable enough to keep me awake. I rubbed my head and tried for a smile. "I really got to get a shower and some sleep. Manny has a girl who works nights. She's as tough as he is and knows the, uh, arrangement. You'll be good until tomorrow."

"Where does a ... guy like you live anyway? You have a family, a house in a nice part of town? Or you have a slick bachelor pad up in one of the new high rises?"

"Don't let the crazy gear fool you. The job is more like a combination club bouncer and sewer inspector than a life of luxury and adventure. The only things James Bond and I have in common are getting punched in the gut, shot at too often, and finding interesting clues in the trash. I've got a tiny place by myself over El Dorado. It's, uh, not far from here. I did have an office, but some local decorators gave it the same treatment your Mercedes got this morning."

"Sounds exciting to me," she said coquettishly. "Bombings, shootings, doing a half-assed job chasing bad guys. And you're single because ... well, the El Dorado ... that's quite a scene, sometimes, or so I've heard. Hey, enjoy! Get something for those Portland taxes, right?"

"Those guys have a ton of fun," I said, "based on the music that makes it through my walls. But nah, I'm just an old-school bachelor I guess."

"Well you're not making your place sound too appealing. Why don't you take a shower and hang out here? Keep an eye on ... things." There was a tease in the last word.

I said I'd take a shower and think about staying. After ten minutes in the palatial marble bathroom, I emerged in a T-shirt, shorts, and a robe. Isabelle was sitting in bed holding what remained of the Voodoo Doll with raspberry-jam-stained fingers.

She motioned to me. "Do you want the last bite?"

I smiled, said thanks, and waved her off. "Good night," I called as I closed the door to the bedroom and headed back out to the parlor. I settled onto the massive couch and fell into the sleep of the dead.

33

It was about nine when I awoke. The door to the bedroom was open and Isabelle was sitting up in bed wearing the hotel robe.

"Hey!" she called out. "Good morning."

I looked around, gathering my wits. All seemed OK. "Good morning," I replied.

"I've been up for a bit. Drank six of these espresso pods." She gestured at the sideboard, where the Presidential Suite featured an Illy X1 Anniversary espresso machine, several steps above the best Nespresso gadgets I'd ever seen.

I looked at the machine, but I was jonesing for the high octane black drip that Manny and I cooked up in the security offices downstairs when we worked late. It was like Isabelle read my mind: "This coffee is … neat … but I wonder if we can find just a big, badass cup of joe? Also: what's the long-term plan, here? Like how long do I need to stay before you or my family or the cops find out who's fucking with me and put a stop to it?"

I paused while I thought about how to answer the latter question.

"Sorry," she added, "I mean this – this is great and I'm very thankful you and Manny set me up here…"

I could hardly blame her – or anyone – for wanting out of the situation, Presidential Suite notwithstanding. "Nah,"

I said. "I totally hear you. Let's start with the coffee. Give me just about ten minutes."

Downstairs, I set about preparing fresh coffee in the security office and considering ways to explain Portland's lack of political stomach for policing. The dim prospect of aggressive action – even for a car bomb – would be incomprehensible to Isabelle, who had grown up in a place that swiftly and firmly demonstrated society's boundaries to any who wandered across them.

When I got back with a couple of venti-sized paper cups, the topic appeared to be moot. Isabelle was dressed – less Hollywood and a lot more PNW this time, in a flannel shirt and jeans – and had her bag packed. She thanked me for the coffee and explained that she'd reserved a car at a rental lot nearby. After tasting the coffee, she thanked me a couple more times. She was heading to OHSU to do "the doctor stuff" that had brought her to town in the first place, then maybe some shopping and back down for an event at the family's vineyard.

We were in the elevator before I could raise an objection. I told her I had a list of Marrenhous properties to run down looking for Fernando and hoped to make some progress by end of day. I apologized again for suggesting her cousin might possibly be a criminal and a fraud.

A moment after we separated in the lobby, she stopped, turned around, and said, "You might want to start by checking out their clubhouse."

"You mean the Pioneers clubhouse?" I asked.

"No, the Marrenhous guys – whenever they were meeting with George's people, or wheeling and dealing with the league or outside investors – they would talk about going back to 'the clubhouse' to talk things over. It's a dive bar in Northwest called The Wreck Room. Apparently they like to hang out there. When business isn't suitable for an office suite, or they want to play the tough guys, they work out of there."

"Hell, why didn't you tell me that in the first place?" I asked.

"I never even heard your name before yesterday?" she threw back as she turned and strode out of the hotel.

My phone told me The Wreck Room had no windows or glass at all and opened at eleven, so I had a few hours if I didn't plan on breaking in blind – and I didn't. I sat in a corner of the hotel lobby, where I could keep an eye on the whole place, drink my coffee, and think about what was next.

34

Next turned out to be a phone call from Peggy: it appeared Jesse was on his way back to Portland and Peggy wanted to give me a heads up.

"He's looking for Tyler. Tyler left a note at the bar when he closed last night. Jesse found it this morning, and he got fired up to chase him to Portland."

"Is he back in *Terminator* mode?" I asked.

"What?"

"Last time he came to town, he rode in on a motorcycle. Seeing him emerge from a cloud of mist and dust with a rifle slung off his back ... it was a bit dramatic, not to mention stupid," I explained.

"Oh, no. He seems less angry now. No rifle. No bike. In fact he's riding up with his sister and said his dirt bike was at your apartment. He wants to pick it up."

"Sounds reasonable. I can meet him and pull out the bike. It's nice of Ashley to come along."

"Actually she was driving up for an interview. She's trying to get a job at a design firm called, I think, Oak Partners. She'll let Jesse off somewhere and then go to her interview."

"OK, thanks," I said, thinking the call was at an end.

"Sure, it's just that..." she began again. "Just that... He said something about Tyler that worried me."

"What? What did he say, Mrs. Owens?"

"He started saying something like, 'He's a goddamn retard sometimes, but he's my goddamn retard. I gotta keep him out of trouble.' Something like that."

"That sounds awfully responsible, looking out for his friend and kin. The language is a little coarse, but…"

"I'm sorry," Peggy said. "I'm afraid I'm not making any sense. Their online friends kept saying Tyler is some kind of retard and not really kin. And that's sorta, technically, true, although I don't think Jesse knows the whole story. Tyler kinda lost it because… Wait. Did you see *The Oregonian*? The league is trying to move the Pioneers. Tyler's whole life is working with Jesse now and without the team… Oh god, I'm messing this all up. I'm sorry. Just try and find the boys before they get into trouble. Isabelle can explain the whole Tyler thing better than I can. I heard you and she spent some … quality time."

"Word travels fast, Mrs. Owens. I was just providing a little security after…"

"After the car bombing. And … overnight. Yes, word does travel fast, Mr. Louis."

I felt my cheeks flush. If I tried to explain, I feared it would only confirm her suspicions.

"OK, thank you, Mrs. Owens. I'll go and meet Jesse."

She hung up.

I left The Multnomah and walked to my building. Instead of going upstairs, I decided to hang out below in the empty gay – but presently not festive – bar.

"Gin or cappuccino, Jack?" Logan asked when I stepped through the open door.

"I'll drink a cappuccino and just stare longingly at the gin bottles," I replied. I wasn't kidding. El Dorado had a dangerously broad collection of quality gin and I always discovered new additions while staring at the shelf.

A few minutes later I was, indeed, drinking the cappuccino and looking at the gin – but also keeping an eye on the entrance in the bar mirror.

A beat up old red Honda Civic pulled to the curb. The front door opened and Jesse unfolded himself out of the compact and stood on the sidewalk in a quilted flannel jacket, jeans, and work boots. Ashley waved to him from the driver seat when he closed the door. I gave Logan a quick salute and walked with my drink to meet Jesse.

He was already at the entrance to the apartments when I called out and he turned. He looked at the coffee, at the door to the bar, back to me.

"Oh, uh, I didn't realize you…" He stopped mid sentence.

I just waited.

"The, uh," he gestured toward the bar entrance, "rainbow flags and stuff."

"You don't have to be gay to get a drink at a gay bar," I said and waited again.

Jesse's face displayed distinct variants of confusion in a slow sequence. At the end, the series began again.

I just walked over and said, "Let's get your bike."

"Yeah, thanks. Wait. How'd you…?"

"Your mom called me and said you were coming this way. And something about looking for Tyler?"

We unlocked the secure storage cage and rolled the bike out.

"Tyler's trying to get himself into trouble and I need to stop him."

"What kind of trouble?"

"It's complicated and I don't understand the whole thing. But, basically, if I'm fucked because the team moves and I can't run the bar, that really sucks. But I thought a lot about what you were saying the other day and… Well, it sucks for me, but for Tyler, it's ten times worse. He has less going for him than I do, let's just say. And then it came out there are these baseball cops – can you believe that? – and some problem with the Pioneers investors and the league is moving the team to fucking Grants Pass. There's gonna be court cases but we're screwed no matter what.

"Tyler said the investors are here, throwing us all under the bus for some deal with the new ballpark. Said he's got nothing to lose and was coming up here with enough lead for everybody. It's crazy. You gotta help me find him."

Jesse was nearly hyperventilating by this point. "So, how do you do it? You're a pro, right? You have some tricks and stuff? How do you track someone down?"

He swung his leg over the bike. I put my hand on his shoulder.

"Honestly, I've been looking for Fernando for days. You and I saw him that one time and I haven't gotten to him since." I didn't mention the clue I planned to follow up on today. Theory of non escalation. "Riding around is probably not gonna be useful if you don't already know where to look. So, if you want to see some tricks of the trade, let's lock the bike, go upstairs, and we'll start where most detective work starts these days: the Internet."

Inside, I set Jesse up with an extra laptop, showed him a few subscription databases, and then opened two blank document windows.

"In addition to the public searches, you can check these databases because you're working as my assistant. You're working as my assistant, right?" He looked at me, slightly confused. I pulled out two twenty dollar bills and put them in front of him. "You're working as my assistant. A, uh contractor, because, ya know. Never mind. Just don't do anything stupid. No stalking girls with my accounts."

He laughed and pointed to the blank documents. "What are these for?"

"One is for everything you can remember about Tyler, focusing on the current situation or the last few days or weeks. The other is for stuff you find out or figure out that might be useful. Stick around here for a bit and grind – I got something to run down."

"OK, thank you, Mr. Louis. You got a Coke? That's all I need and I'm gonna lock in."

"Help yourself to whatever's in the fridge," I said. It wouldn't be much.

I took a quick shower, put on some hiking pants with cargo pockets, my T-shirt body armor under a shell that featured internal storage and abrasion resistance, and a pair of decent trail shoes.

Jesse appeared hard at work sans Coke, but happy having unearthed an ancient Dr. Pepper. I left the apartment and walked north, headed for a bus to The Wreck Room.

35

I hadn't walked in – just eyeballed the building as I came down the block – and, even for a dive, this place looked rough. Filthy clapboard siding covered the upper floor of the two-story building: apartments or storage. The main floor had an alcove in shabby decorative-stone facade around the entrance and mildewed clapboard elsewhere. A broken picnic bench chained to the sidewalk offered space to sit and smoke.

Inside the steel door, a dropped ceiling gave the impression of a stuffy and claustrophobic basement rec room, presumably the inspiration for the establishment's punny name. Fake wood siding, formica booths, lottery game machines, pinball, and promo beer merch filled out the area I entered. To my right was the bar proper and, beyond that, a cave of pool tables illuminated by cheap workshop fluorescents. A number of TVs showed sports through a haze of vape and ganja.

I picked up a Rainier tallboy and wandered around, ostensibly looking at the game machines, then the billiards players. I scoped the people and the place, looking for any kind of back office – or, hell, a front office. Two chunky guys in the corner kept an eye on me the while.

Sitting down at the bar, I didn't want to make anyone nervous, so I stared at a ballgame and listened to patrons chatter. A man in a Buffalo cap with greasy curls and a dirty

T-shirt added a fourth Modelo bottle to the stack in front of him before the barmaid collected the empties. She disappeared into a nook between the bar and the front wall of the place. That spot seemed an unlikely size and location to hide any kind of meeting room and my supposition was confirmed when she returned from it carrying a plastic basket of thin fries for the Bills fan.

The two seemed to know each other, drifting comfortably in and out of conversation on a miscellany of personal topics. The man's girl had left rehab and refused to come home until there was booze on offer. He had driven around Portland for twelve hours before finding her on the street. The barkeep shared a similar tale about a roommate.

When the keg of Blue Moon kicked, I took the opportunity to ask about a basement.

"Beer lines go down to kegs in the basement?"

Apparently not: "I wish," said the barmaid. "No basement in this place so we got two kegs under the end of the bar over there," the girl said, pointing toward the door. "The other two are in the kitchen. I gotta wrestle the Blue Moon outta the fridge and roll a new one in from back there." This time she gestured toward an empty side room that looked like a place you could reserve for a party. In the back, I could see the line of stacked kegs.

I took one more quick walk around looking for doors, obvious or otherwise, that might lead to any back room, upstairs, downstairs, Shanghai tunnel … and saw nothing. There was another approach. On my phone, I pulled up Portland Maps, the city's public, unified, and extraordinarily detailed GIS application, on which the exact outline and area of every building was visible. Was it the spirit of open records? Or merely part of the tax extraction machinery? Either way, my phone measured and diagrammed the interior of the bar and I overlaid that on the Portland Maps outline. The bar had two restrooms and the building had an extra chunk of space adjoining the men's of about equal size.

So I headed a place I hadn't yet searched, took a leak, and picked the lock on what appeared to be a janitorial supply closet. There were the usual metal shelves, drain cleaner, a mop in a rolling galvanized bucket, plunger, random tools … and, since I now knew to look for it, the faint outline of another door at the back of the closet. That door did not have a visible lockset, so I ran the blade of my Swiss army knife along the gap until I felt the bolt. It wasn't a deadbolt and was well lubed: it slid easily under the blade. A tiny bit of pressure moved the door slightly and made no noise.

Going in blind meant prepping for a grand entrance. I turned to secure the blade with my other hand so I could have my gun ready, took a breath, and threw the door.

36

I caught a limited impression of a large, brightly lit room with several men around a card table. Most of the view, however, was obscured by an additional man, standing right in front of me. I hadn't even registered his face, when my eyes tracked a massive fist coming at me. The fist smashed into my head before I could complete a thought.

I fell back into the closet but the ogre who had slammed me wasn't done. He grabbed my jacket, pulled me up, turned me ninety degrees, and pinned me against the doorframe. I felt hands grab at me, taking my gun and phone. Enfeebled by the strong grip he still had on my clothes, I wrenched to toss a weak punch at the man's abdomen.

I kicked at his shin, stomped his foot. He didn't react. Just slowly turned me and then smashed me into the brick wall inside the closet. Maybe he closed the door or maybe I just blacked out.

The darkness was only momentary, a conclusion I drew when my eyes opened onto the same large man dragging me along the floor. He pulled me across the space and threw me so that I was lying on the floor with my back to the wall.

"Get him up!" a deep voice growled from across the card table.

The big man moved aggressively toward me but I feebly waved him off and propped myself up against the wall.

The deep voice slowly got to his feet, using a quad cane. While he rose, I looked around and took in two additional men: a sleazy-looking thin guy with curly hair in a jean jacket and, sitting across from him, Fernando Nuñez.

"What are you doing here with these guys, Fernando?" I managed to ask before the guy with the cane reached me, snapped out a collapsible baton, and took a swipe at my ribs. I think I'd rather be shot than whacked with one of those batons.

"You shut up until we ask you a question," the man said. "Fernando just wants what's best for his ball club and also for its owners. Right? And what's best is the biggest owner – Mr. George – signing onto our project. But Mr. George, he just isn't convinced. So we've been working with his star pitcher here to, uh, make the case."

"How's that working out for you?" I asked, and got another jab in the ribs from the baton in recompense for my snark.

Fernando spoke up: "It's not gonna work out at all *por los mamagüevos aqui.*"

The bull who had clocked me on entering now turned to Fernando, suddenly enraged, screaming, "No one asked you, you piece of shit!"

Fernando stood to square up against this guy. Fernando was taller by several inches but the other man was wider by a foot. A boxing match broke out as the men traded blows. Then the big guy reached around to his back and his fist came up with a spiked knuckle duster. He slammed it into Fernando's shoulder. Fernando screamed a curse I didn't understand and took a falling step back, grabbing his shoulder, which was already bleeding through his jersey.

The poor kid's pitching arm was gonna be a mess after this, assuming we got out of here at all.

When the bull leaned in for a followup, his jacket rode up revealing a gun in the back of his waistband – something black and compact. Pulling myself together and figuring I'd only have one chance, I sprung forward and launched headfirst at the small of the man's back. My hands were outstretched. I became a running back diving for – it turned out – a Glock 30. The pistol came away in my hands and as I hit the floor and rolled, I saw the hulking shadow of the man, knuckleduster silhouetted against the fluorescent ceiling light. The weapon had sprouted a concealed blade and as it began its journey toward me, I launched four chunks of lead in the caliber of our Lord.

The agency in the man's attack was arrested but gravity continued to bring his 250-odd pounds down on top of me. The knife struck harmlessly, embedded in the vinyl-tiled floor to my left. While I fought to free myself from the mass of bleeding man, my ears still ringing from the percussion of the shots, I heard all hell break out among the two other hostiles.

A long time ago, I was a high school wrestler – a mediocre one. But when the opponent is literally a corpse, I can hold my own and I did so, flipping my erstwhile attacker off of me and springing up from the floor. I aimed at the thin, younger, and more mobile man, expecting he'd be quicker on the attack than the man with the cane. The younger man's hands scrambled around his waistband and in and out of his pockets. He was looking for a weapon and couldn't find it. I was certain he had the worst intentions but I didn't see a gun or even a knife in his hand … yet. He hadn't even charged me; I couldn't fire on the unarmed man. Before I could pivot the Glock off him, a donkey's kick to the sternum threw me backward against the wall. As I slumped down, I seemed to hear the report of the older man's shiny, blued .357 S&W.

Intellectually, I knew I'd be OK: I was wearing "T-shirt type" flexible body armor under my clothes and a normal handgun round wouldn't penetrate. That didn't make it any less painful; nor did it change the laws of physics so I could escape the 500-plus ft.-lbs. of energy the round carried.

The man approached but didn't fire again. I was slowly catching my breath when I realized I was soaked with the first man's blood. Lying at the base of the wall, I decided to play the part and not risk a second shot to my unarmored lower abdomen ... or head.

I hammed it up, gurgling and rolling my eyes a little.

The man turned away, toward the thin young guy. The S&W dangled in his hand. "This is the asshole who was sneaking around Chuck's boat, right?"

"Yeah, that's him."

"Some kind of cop?"

"Pretty sure he's no kind of cop. He still breathing? You want me to finish him?"

My eyes went wide at the realization my stealth op on the boat had apparently been less than stealthy and also at the absurd size of the Glock 17L the kid had finally extricated from his pants. With a slide half the length of his thigh, his hand slightly shaking as he turned it forty-five degrees, the gun and its wielder momentarily made a parody of Samuel L. Jackson's executioner scene in *Pulp Fiction*.

I turned a spontaneous laugh into a theatrical gurgle and spit some phlegm.

Then I slid my hand out, still holding the bull's .45 and fired three times at the kid. The old man regained his grip on the .357 but had the long, heavy double-action pull to deal with whereas I had only the Austrian striker to wrangle. The next and last three rounds in the .45 struck him as I fired into his lower abdomen on a steep chestward trajectory.

Fernando was huddling in the corner, clutching his arm as blood continued to flow. I needed to get him to a hospital – a good one if he had any hope of pitching again.

No one from the bar had penetrated the back office, likely under strict orders. Who knew what the patrons thought was going on? In most cities, this many gunshots would have drawn the cops, but Portland's culture made it more like living in the country: if the law came at all, it'd be half an hour getting here.

I collected my gun and phone and began planning an exit for Fernando and myself. I was alright but he needed an emergency department. We'd have to get a rideshare outside the central city if we wanted to skip a queue of bums and head cases.

Such were the mental calculations I made as I ordered the car, applied a makeshift tourniquet to Fernando's arm, and covered him with the old man's sport coat, thankfully left on the back of his chair and blood free.

To hide my extremely bloody appearance, the best I could come up with was stripping off my shirt and half wearing the young man's ill-fitting jacket.

We left by the push-bar exit door in the building's back wall and stumbled to the corner to wait for our ride. When the silver Tesla silently pulled up, the driver was on a call and messing with the app so he didn't clock our sketchy appearance. When I got the rear door open, his face turned to panic. "You guys can't get in!" he yelled. But the door was already open and he didn't stomp the accelerator. I reached in with a wad of cash.

"We won't be any trouble. Just need a ride to the hospital. You know how the ambulances are."

The driver nodded. The county's ego had driven ambulances to near zero, a case of political inside baseball breaking out. Injured normies knew to call a rideshare or they'd die waiting, a vision of a pol's smarmy grin in their mind's eye.

We slid into the back seat and closed the door. The driver was about to pull away when the tiny jacket I was half wearing slid off my arm, revealing massive amounts of blood.

"Oh no. You gotta get out! Now! No ride."

This ride was non-negotiable. I waved the empty Glock 30. "Drive," I growled. And off we went.

After I talked the ED staff down from their excitement over my appearance, they got to work with Fernando. They stabilized him easily and admitted him for surgery on the arm. I stayed long enough to get Altagracia on the phone, the team doctor, and finally George himself, who said he'd be there within the hour.

George arrived genuinely torn up. He seemed to feel he was responsible; he said he just couldn't go along with all the schemes that were brewing. He mentioned the car bombing as well and I explained that Isabelle was OK but also that – unlike in Fernando's case – the culprit in the bombing was still unknown. George then got on the blower, trying to round up sports docs from Tigard all the way to San Francisco.

I headed to the cafeteria, where they didn't appreciate the morale boost that junk food could provide in a clinical setting. I was stuck with a gooey vegetable wrap and coffee that tasted like nylon. I took it outside and summoned a rideshare back to the city.

37

From the car, I called Jesse to see how the search for Tyler was going.

"I finally got a lead on him!" Jesse said.

"Congrats! So the online sleuthing paid off?" I asked.

"No. I actually got a call from his mom. I think you did too, but she said you weren't answering."

"Yeah, things got a little crazy. Sorry."

"Bonnie said Tyler wants to talk to some people who work for Multnomah County. It's weird. I don't understand what connection he has with them. Before I could look into it, though, I had to leave to meet Ash. Her interview went to shit. She called, crying, from a place called the Rialto, so I'm on my way there."

"What happened? Is she alright?" I asked.

The Rialto Pool Room was the latest incarnation of a Portland site legendary for gambling, Prohibition-era booze, prostitution, organized crime, and corrupt officials. It was entirely unclear what Ashley would be doing there unless she'd just wandered in, looking for the nearest bar or bathroom. My speculation wasn't far from the truth.

"I think so – it sounds like it wasn't what she expected. The job was assistant. She thought assistant artist or art director, but it was literally sitting outside the office, answering the phone and keeping hobos out of the lobby. She had better experience and a way better portfolio than the people there but they blew her off. They had an art position open but wouldn't talk to her about it, not sure why. She even talked with the senior partner about her work in LA, new software, AI. It didn't go well."

"Touchy about the AI thing?" I ventured.

"Nah, they didn't understand what she was talking about. Kinda out of touch. I didn't get how they have clients. Ash sent me some links and their work is half-assed next to hers. She's really good, ya know." The pride was audible in Jesse's voice. "Turns out they keep contracting with the government and some kinda nonprofits, redoing the same work every year and billing for it. In the end, they didn't offer her any job at all, said she didn't align with their mission or some shit. She had a drink and asked me to meet her at the bar."

"The Rialto?"

"Yeah, she said it was a little sketchy."

"It's not the worst. But it's good of you to go down there. Tell her not to sweat the art job. It's Portland. If they didn't do it, it doesn't exist. If they did it and it's no good, then the taxpayers cover it. In its own way, it's no more crooked than the business in LA," I mused, before adding, "Except, of course, that films actually get made and sometimes people pay to see 'em." My own cynicism was getting to me.

I checked my phone during the remainder of the ride into Portland. Bonnie had indeed left a message about Tyler. She found a ton of notes about the county in his room. She sounded surprisingly worried but didn't provide enough info for me to figure out why. I tried returning the call, with no luck.

I mused on the paradox of Oregon's arrested development as we crawled through congestion. The state excelled in pre-industrial activities – from hops and berries, grapes and hazelnuts to logging, hunting, and grazing, you really couldn't do better. From the crops and game they got as far as beer, wine, and food, and aced those too. But it stopped there. Semiconductors fizzled; software and services never worked. When pros like Ashley showed up with expertise, they got frozen out of corrupt, small-town cliques LARPing business.

The car pulled up outside El Dorado and I prepared to get out when my phone buzzed. Ashley had not been at the Rialto when Jesse got there. What should he do?

I texted him, said him I'd get there ASAP. A wad of literally bloody twenty-dollar bills got my driver to log off his app, wait ten minutes for me to run inside and shower the mess off and then take me over.

38

When I got out of the car at the Rialto, Jesse was standing by the entrance, talking with club security and demanding to know why they kicked Ashley out of the place. Security claimed they hadn't thrown Ashley out. They said that another patron had asked her to leave and she did. It sounded fishy, so I told Jesse to circle the block, show her pic from his phone's photo album to the loiterers "hanging out," and ask if they'd seen her.

While Jesse set off on his assignment, I attempted a more aggressive, but less public, conversation with the pool room's bouncers. They didn't open up and kept looking nervously toward the bartender, so I switched gears and took it up with him. Another couple of twenties — these with less blood — along with my investigator ID card got me a bit more of the story.

It turned out Ashley was on her third drink and had started wandering around the largely empty bar when she got curious about a woman playing video poker. The gambler resembled a chubby middle-aged librarian and was pounding buttons on a poker machine while three security men in dark suits orbited around her. Ashley had accidentally stumbled onto the county's most infamous political leader a dozen drinks and a couple hours into a binge. Worse, these weren't Oregon Lottery poker machines but the real thing: illegal and with a lot more money on the line.

Most of Portland knew the commissioner as a slow-witted, emotionally stunted, and maladroit puppet for more capable political operators. Only a few knew that – as her credibility had slid alongside that of Multnomah County – she had transitioned from good wine to bad wine then to bad liquor and from charity bingo to lottery games and thence to underground machines where she could lose money fast enough to get in real trouble. Rumor was that her house was in foreclosure and taxpayers were bailing her out, but no one could get close enough to ask since she bought a personal security detail on the public dime as well.

Personally, I'd always felt a bit bad for her. She reminded me of a sick dog whose owner kicked it for peeing on the rug: she neither understood anything about her job nor had any capacity to do better. She just botched everything, kept getting kicked, and had turned to booze and gambling to dull the pain. Empathy aside, it was not a flattering picture of one of Oregon's most powerful people, so her security tried to keep it from view. In this case, that meant words with Ashley and showing her the door.

I looked at the security footage: although they did put hands on her to urge her out, it didn't appear rough and she walked away from the Rialto on her own.

By the time I learned this much, Jesse had completed his circuit of the block and returned with nothing to report. I suggested taking the next block, closer to the river. We'd go together.

We made it down Alder and around the corner to Third when we spotted her.

Ashley was sitting on a filthy scrap of cardboard in the entrance to an empty storefront, crying. Blood covered her hands, face, and the silk blouse she had worn for her interview. Jesse got down next to her on the ground, put his arms around her, and held her as she began to sob.

A couple of minutes later, he helped her to her feet. She looked a mess but wasn't badly injured: her nose, a cut near her ear, and another near her lip provided a surprising amount of blood.

Ashley confirmed that no one at the Rialto had roughed her up – they had just sent her on her way a bit drunk and disoriented. Here on Third, a homeless woman had asked her for money. She wanted to give the woman ten dollars but accidentally gave her a twenty-dollar bill as well and when she asked for it back, a yelling match ensued.

"The crazy lady did this to you?" Jesse asked, incensed.

"No, she didn't do anything, just yelled a little and walked away. This other guy rolled up on a skateboard, in a black hoodie, wearing a mask. He screamed at me. I didn't even know what he was saying. He hit me with the skateboard and I fell. I just … ended up here," she explained.

"OK," I said. "Let's go to my place. You can rest and get cleaned up. I don't have any women's clothes, but…"

Jesse jumped in: "I bet they got plenty downstairs!"

"Jesus Christ, Jesse. It's a gay bar. Not a drag bar. They're not the same thing. Never mind…"

I called yet another rideshare and once again distracted the driver with cash while we tried to keep blood off the upholstery. In my tiny apartment, Ashley showered and cleaned up and then Jesse and I applied disinfecting solution and bandages.

"The ear and nose will be fine, but this cut by your lip… If you don't want to look like a gangster, probably should get this stitched by someone competent," I suggested.

"Can we go to a doctor or a hospital near here?" she asked.

It wasn't the right time to explain why she'd never get treated in Portland. "Just too busy," I oversimplified. "If you head back home, they'll take care of you in Newberg, do a better job of it too. I'm really sorry. I feel awful that your interview in the city went this way."

Jesse gave me a look and I was afraid he'd launch into a torrent of possibly accurate, but inopportune, commentary on the state of the world. I shot him a sharp look back.

"Why don't you drive your sister home? Help her get to a doc there. Try to keep your parents from losing their minds when they hear what happened."

He looked over at my computer, where his database searches and several map views were still open. I put my hand on his shoulder. "I'll look into Tyler and see what I can find. Once your sister is home, come right back and we can work on this thing together, try and sort it out."

His face showed him thinking it over.

"Talk to Bonnie while you're there," I suggested. I hoped he'd keep his cool and thought some encouragement wouldn't hurt: "I know you'll be able to stay chill and reassure her that we're looking out for Tyler. You can give her my card, too."

We sat uncomfortably in the hot space and swigged a couple of icy beers apiece. As my adrenaline receded, the pain from my earlier struggle at The Wreck Room made itself known.

Darkness slowly fell. Jesse left and came back with Ashley's car. I helped her in. I watched the Civic roll off toward Union Station on the way to the freeway ramp.

I felt pretty good to have found Fernando and pulled loose at least one thread of the Marrenhous plot. Not a perfect outcome, but one we could live with. I'd earned a decent night's sleep and intended to redeem it forthwith.

39

I woke up to a bright, clear day, sunlight streaming in before eight despite the earth's irresistible autumn advance around the sun. My phone had a message from Altagracia thanking me again for my help and saying she was on her way to Portland from the D.R. to help her boy. She hoped to see me when she was here.

As for the sketchy baseball deals, landlords, and county crooks, there was no putting any of that toothpaste back in the tube. A thorough cleanup was unlikely and, anyway, would require FBI work since the would-be local defendants owned the courts by way of orchestrated judicial retirements.

I couldn't clear the air of the general stench. But, if I got lucky, I might be able to disentangle some good guys from bad ones and buy another chance for the extended Delany family.

I also needed to get some insight into Tyler's situation. To my pleasure, roads to both of those goals seemed to run through Isabelle. It turned out she'd stayed another night in Portland, albeit not at The Multnomah. I invited her for breakfast to a favorite spot, a tiny bubble of another era suspended in the fluid of the present: Nick's Cafe.

While I drank coffee and waited for Isabelle, I phoned Hannah for an update on the timeline of the feds' assault on "Oscar." The news was not good. A group of special agents from the FBI, DEA, BATFE, some marshals, and a whole pile of lawyers would be here "soon." Hannah didn't know when soon was and, hell, I'm sure she couldn't tell me if she did. But we were talking days at most. I knew enough to track Robbie O'Shea and squeeze him. But the involved electeds and their staff were basically white-collar mob: they didn't leave big ugly piles of steaming clue about their exploits where I could find them. I'd have to get creative.

While I was thinking about options, the door swung open. I hadn't been certain that Isabelle would make it through the grime a typical night ejaculated onto the streets of Old Town, so I was relieved to see her stroll in. She had it together appearance-wise – hair pulled back, jacket over a cashmere top, blue jeans, and boots – but her attitude was perturbed.

"There's a guy. Right. Out. There. In a wheelchair, smoking drugs, surrounded by an enormous nest of shit… Well, trash but also, literally, shit. And he's blowing smoke in the face of anyone who approaches the door. I don't get it. How does Nick – is this Nick, here?" she asked, gesturing toward the old Greek man in the kitchen. "How does he even stay in business?"

"Lemme see if I can help," I said, and texted a cop friend to ask if he could move the addict along and get the sidewalk cleaned up. "He'll offer the guy all kinds of social help, too," I explained. That was the Portland protocol – but odds were, the dude would rather be high across the street in a different pile of filth than halfway sober in a decent apartment. "Meanwhile, activists said apartments were inhumane: it was a human right to have a million-dollar house and we were abusing our privilege by taking away their dope." I couldn't help but smile, thinking of my own little apartment as a human-rights violation. It was too early in the morning to contemplate the mobius-loop thinking of the local clown class.

I turned the conversation in a cheerier direction, pointing out the legit vintage fixtures of the coffee shop: style and functionality that had never failed and never warranted replacement, going on sixty years.

"The prices are about sixty years old too," Isabelle said, both surprised and delighted. "And the architecture all around this block is even better."

"Yeah, Portland's always had a different set of problems, but underneath there's still a current that connects it to Yamhill and the rest. Which reminds me of something I wanted to ask about," I said.

We paused our conversation to order and to marvel at the platters that Nick's wife set in front of customers at a neighboring booth.

"So Jesse's struggling a bit. He's taken it on the chin trying to grow up fast," I began. "But Tyler… It seems to be his turn to panic. I get that Jesse's his best friend and best hope for employment, there's some stuff to sort out there, and some guys have talked shit about him. But it doesn't totally add up for me. There's gotta be some other reason he's freaking out. And what kind of mission brought him to the city?"

"Wait. What? Tyler's here in Portland?"

"I'm not one hundred percent sure. Bonnie said something about the county – er, Multnomah County – actually. I'm in the dark."

Our food arrived along with an ephemeral brightening of Isabelle's visage at the appearance of omelettes, toast, and hash browns. But the moment faded. Her eyes fell and she almost put her face in her hands, hesitating at the last second: a trained reflex to avoid messing up her makeup.

"You always worry that some big crisis will tear open an old wound, you know?"

I didn't know where she was going, so I just held my coffee mug and looked intently at her, listening.

She went on. "My sister and Jake adopted Tyler when he was a year old. He's got some learning disabilities and social issues, as you've probably noticed."

"I'd heard something but, honestly, hadn't noticed, myself. He tossed out a couple of immature lines like lots of teenage boys do. Anyway, he seems more with it than most of our city council." It sounded like a joke. I was not joking.

"He's got some challenges," Isabelle began. "And the biggest ones are financial and emotional. Because of estate decisions made generations ago, he can't inherit any of our family's money or directly participate in our investments. You can imagine: as an orphan, that only made him feel worse, like a permanent outsider. Being part of Jesse's business meant so much. And then Reggie giving him a piece of the place? – Reggie could do that, it was all his – well, Tyler felt like he had a future and was really part of the family and the town. I know it sounds awful to say it like this. But we were all doing the best we could."

"I think I get it," I began.

Isabelle jumped in. "I'm worried about that 'county' remark. Tyler's parents… Where do I start? Tyler's dad had been in prison. They let him out during Covid but then he died – OD'd in Eugene. His mom had died years earlier in the state hospital. It was fucked up. A lot of things went wrong. Tyler always blamed this one county commissioner who was involved in sending her to the hospital. A lot of people messed up, but also there wasn't – hell, there still isn't – a better place. Doesn't make it any less personal to Tyler, though. Especially since the commissioner was a Perescelli. Perescelli like that big-ass plaque on the museum. Untouchable family and, let's be honest, a bit full of themselves, off in their own world. That was Greg Perescelli, father of Mary Perescelli."

"Who is currently a commissioner," I finished the thought. "So that's who he came to see."

"That would figure."

I looked at my watch. "The full commission meeting starts in fifteen minutes. We can try to intercept him there." I mentally calculated. "If you're willing to break some traffic laws, we can take Jesse's dirt bike."

"I heard there are no traffic laws in Portland," Isabelle smirked.

We paid and left Nick's. On our way out, we passed a patrol unit. The cop was on the sidewalk half urging, half pleading with the fentanyl smoker, asking what he needed and what the cop could do to help him move. A twenty-something in anarchist teen-rebel garb rolled by on a skateboard, spit at the cop, and screamed, "Leave 'em alone, fucking pig!" as he turned the corner.

"Then again, maybe whatever Portland and Yamhill had in common is just gone," Isabelle said. I gestured and we took off toward my place at a half jog.

Three minutes later, she was mounted precariously behind me on the bike as we roared down Fifth Avenue toward Madison, briefly slowed to turn the corner, then blasted onto the Hawthorne Bridge at well over twice the posted limit.

40

We entered the county building just as the public, journalists, lobbyists, and staff were settling into the commission chamber. I spotted Tyler right away, sitting not far from the entrance. The commissioners hadn't arrived yet.

Tyler got up and walked to the far end of the room. He was fidgeting with something under his clothes. Behind me, I heard people greeting – and attempting to buttonhole – the commissioners on their way in. Tyler's hand went under his shirt and I watched him rest it on the grip of a pistol.

He walked toward us.

I stepped forward briskly, covering the distance and buying a few seconds.

"Hey buddy! Remember me? Helping Jesse out with stuff at the bar?"

He didn't quite recognize me but he stood still.

"Come with me, man, we gotta talk."

I put my arm around him. He was stronger due to his youth, but I had physical leverage and training. I kept my arm between his and the gun, gave him a hug and a hearty thump on the back, and guided him away from the entering politicos.

As soon as they passed us, I subtly but forcibly led him out of the chamber and through the main doors to the street.

"What is this?" I asked, taking a peek. "You're not gonna sort anything out with a .357, Tyler."

"What the hell do you know?" he shot back.

"I know you're pissed. And… Look, these guys – and gals – are in a heap of shit with the feds, with some local heavyweights, and… Just take it easy and hopefully they get what they deserve."

He was fired up. "Who the fuck are you? You don't know anything about … anything! This isn't about working at Jesse's bar. These motherfuckers fucked my whole life up."

"You've been waiting a long time for this … this chance to talk to the commissioner, right?"

"Goddamned right I have," he replied.

"And, like you said, things are pretty messed up right now. So, if I can get you a meeting to discuss this – conversation, not weaponry – would you be able to wait a day or two?"

He hesitated. His face was still flushed and I could see the muscles tensing as he considered making a break for it.

I looked down, stayed calm and kept an eye on his feet. If he pivoted to rabbit, I'd have to do something.

After an excruciating thirty seconds or so, he said, "Yeah, sure. Jesse taught me some things when we would go hunting. About waiting out your prey. Maybe it works like that here too."

"That's a solid lesson," I agreed. "How about you hang out in Portland with your Aunt Isabelle for a day or two and I'll try and make something happen?"

Tyler's eyes lit up and then clouded over again just as fast. "I don't have the cash right now. This town is expensive."

"Don't worry about that. I've got a hookup," I said.

I found Isabelle at the back of the commission chamber and we all synced up. I'd get them a room at The Multnomah – probably not as fancy as she had enjoyed previously, but with fully functioning utilities – and they'd hang out while I tried to get the Delany project disentangled from the Marrenhous play and the Oscar scam. If I was lucky, by the time the FBI came crashing into the county, George, Isabelle, Jesse, and the rest of their families would look more like the victims they were than the perpetrators they almost became. If I got really lucky, there might even be an opportunity for the kids in there somewhere.

I phoned Manny at The Multnomah and he answered, "Reservations."

"OK, wise ass," I replied.

"You mean you're not calling to get a room for someone on the down low? Again?"

"Well, yeah. If you put it that way, maybe we should set up a loyalty program or something."

"The loyalty program is you get to play house dick this weekend, 2 p.m. to 2 a.m., Friday and Saturday and, if we're lucky, no one dies in the place."

That was, more or less, the arrangement we'd long had, so I told him if he brewed the coffee and fetched the donuts, he had a deal. "In the meantime, would you have a suite, or at least two adjoining rooms?" I asked sheepishly.

"As long as … whoever … is out by the weekend, you can count on it. We're dead over here. Management won't let me mess with the Presidential Suite this early in the day or for more than one night. But a regular corner suite is yours, complete with a delightful city view of fetty and fornication."

I signed off and asked Tyler if he'd be up for riding the dirt bike back across the river. Isabelle and I took the bus and walked the rest of the way. We found Tyler marveling at the lobby, the bike already in the parking garage where the valet had told him to stash it.

Manny Gil strolled up, looked at me, looked at Isabelle, looked back at me, and broke into a wide grin. I gave him a side-eye that warned it away. Manny and I sorted the details and got some keys for Isabelle and Tyler. It was a fair guess Tyler had never been in a hotel this opulent in his life.

I called Bonnie and then Jesse, giving each of them a redacted account of what had transpired. Jesse asked if he could come back to town and help at all. A moment's thought suggested he wouldn't add much besides risk. I asked how Ashley was and he said OK, but that she wanted to be left alone. A second moment's thought reminded me Jesse needed to feel useful, to be kept out of trouble, and at the least he could help keep an eye on Tyler and Isabelle while I took a swing at Oscar. The young man was audibly thrilled and said he'd be at the hotel in an hour, give or take.

Meantime, I bought lunch and drinks for everyone, mentally hoping George would reimburse me before the credit card bill was due. Theo Harrison, who'd taught me about insurance fraud, was fond of saying, "It's hard to sell fifty-dollar whiskey for a hundred dollars. And if a man succeeds at it for long, he's more likely a crook than a business genius." Theo, however, was talking wholesale and not the eye-watering markups of hotel bars. Tyler was amused that the fanciest bar in the place was called The Yamhill Room. Clearly, he said, whoever put the hotel up had never visited his town. I took him for a stroll around the room where we looked at the massive scenic Oregon oil paintings. Two of them illustrated the narrow gauge railroad named for the Yamhill River, but which never got closer to Tyler's hometown than Newberg.

I got Isabelle and Tyler settled in their suite – truly a nice room if not for the junkies thirty feet below the balcony – and texted the info to Jesse. It was a regular family reunion when he strolled in half an hour later with a brown paper bag full of beers.

"Let's bring those with us," I said to Jesse, before he could crack one and kick back.

"Bring them where?" he asked.

"We've got some brainstorming to do," I explained.

"Like in your little apartment? Wouldn't it be nicer to do it here?"

"Bring the beer. Come with me. I've got a better place in mind."

Tyler was playing with the hotel infotainment system. I waved meaningfully to Isabelle. Jesse and I got his car from the valet.

41

Thirty-five minutes later, Jesse and I were sitting in a canoe off Ross Island. The Multnomah's parent company had a sister property – more modern in all ways good and bad – on the west bank of the Willamette and we helped ourselves to one of their boats.

A period of vigorous paddling let us blow off some steam and put us on the east side of the island, where the city was no longer visible and the distant shum of traffic on the bridges might have been the wind. We stopped paddling for a bit and floated closer to the island, where we caught sight of a pair of massive bald eagles. One of them settled on a log at water level while the other circled and suddenly dived toward us, plummeting to the river and rising back up with a fish in its talons. Jesse and I reflexively ducked, even though the bird was at least fifty feet away. The sight was breathtaking.

"I'll have to tell the folks at home they haven't paved over everything here just yet," Jesse joked.

"The folks *here* aren't sure they want a city at all and to prove it they haven't paved a damned thing in years," I shot back.

"So what do we do now? Wait for an idea or something? Drink beer?" Jesse asked, reaching for the bag.

"Not the worst plan," I said, catching and opening a can he tossed my way.

"I get why people would come here," he began. "To a city, I mean. Like Ashley going to Los Angeles. You can just do what you want, and if it doesn't work, you can try something else. In the country, you're stuck. Baseball and beer was too good to be true. You grow hazelnuts… I guess if you're lucky you can make some cash doing grapes. It's crazy work and you can still end up with a jungle or washed out mud instead of a vineyard. Lots of risk, not much reward. There's more here. I can see that."

"Grass is greener, I guess," I replied. "People doing whatever they can for a buck is how Fernando got kidnapped and why I had to shoot three people yesterday. Plenty of weeding and pruning needed in the city, too."

"Those guys totally deserved to get shot."

I thought about this for a moment.

"I'd just say the alternative is not something I could tolerate. I mean Fernando and myself getting killed. One nice thing about this job: I don't have to worry about what people deserve. If I shoot, it's because someone needs shooting. Cops and judges worry about what's deserved, and I wouldn't want their jobs. I used to work in insurance fraud and we did a lot of weeding there too, although usually with a computer and only rarely with weapons."

"I'm jealous, I gotta say. It must be nice to be established and have your whole life kind of sorted out. It's scary when you're just getting started these days."

"If I were an AI, you know what I'd say to that? I'd say life always feels that way when you're young. Or I'd say I haven't really figured things out, that I'm always learning. Or I'd say that when I was your age I felt the same and when you're my age, you'll have things figured out too. AI drives me crazy sometimes because it's like being trapped in a Hallmark store. You ever been to one of those? Never mind. My point is, you're half right. There's no greeting card answer. You're always making little corrections, or big corrections, worrying they're not the right ones or they're in the wrong direction. You take your hand off the wheel and you're royally screwed." I laughed a little. "It does get easier, won't lie about that, but it's still a Sisyphean task."

"Then where's this smooth, happy path? Middle-class life, everything working out? Where's that come from for anybody?"

"I think when it comes at all, it's the outcome of the process – like the eagles and the fish here, the killer pinot coming out of Carlton, or an epic Pioneers game – balance of opposing forces. And I don't mean peaceful balance, I mean vicious fight-to-the-death. Sometimes that balance becomes visible with time and distance."

"What if it doesn't work out? Like, it seems a lot of the time it just doesn't?"

"Well, if it never works out, we're not here talking about it. Or maybe those aren't the stories we're interested in. It's survivorship bias. Not sure if we pick the stories or the stories pick us."

"I guess. We've been getting our asses kicked. My whole family, I mean. But that's sure as hell not the story I want to tell. Still don't know what we can do to make a difference right now, though, with everything going on."

I put my paddle in the river and suddenly I had an answer, or at least something to try. We finished our beers and started back around the island just as an autumn storm blew in. It took a little longer than expected to get to shore and we were soaked and exhausted when we got there.

"Once we get cleaned up, are you down for a little investigative interviewing?" I asked Jesse.

"Of course," he replied. "Who are we interviewing?"

"Her," I said, showing him my phone, where I was writing a text to Abby Sparrow.

42

I'd offered to come straight to wherever, and the quirky dive on Southeast Grand was the spot she named. Although I had dried off, I still felt a chill from the river and set about fighting it with a massive bowl of clam chowder.

We were served by a woman named Ronnie who was Portland weird in a truly old-school way. She was friendly, competent, and – based on some comments she tossed off about the fearsome street scene on the other side of Southeast Grand, plenty tough. I didn't know what Jesse would make of her – probably confirmation of some wretched stereotypes – but I knew something he didn't: this woman had seen and lived things long before they became popular in Los Angeles middle schools, or a way to get TikTok fans. Long before she could expect the normies to offer a smile or shrug instead of a threat and a switchblade, even in Portland.

"Here's to doing the thing when it's hard," I said and toasted Abby and Jesse with my Old Town Lager. The beer complemented the clam chowder exquisitely.

"I remembered seeing a reference to Oscar when I skimmed your older blogs," I began, addressing Abby. "I'm thinking someone – or some *ones* – at the county have recycled aliases or fallen in love with their scam a bit too much. Something to do with a Native American project?" I asked.

"Oh my god," began Abby, "it's beyond ridiculous, even for here, and yeah I might know where Oscar's filing cabinet lives. A few years ago, there was a project to turn over land near the confluence of the Willamette and the Columbia to a group of Native Americans. They represented tribes who had been displaced along the river the last couple centuries. I covered it because it had potential to impact the rivers and development. It looked like a no-lose: a boon to the Native groups – real land and wealth – and it would meet the needs of Portland's growing economy. Then the county commissioners – well, three of them – decided they didn't like the design. Three middle-aged white ladies said they expected the Natives to build an interpretive center and a mock village and put on some kinda leather-and-feather cultural shows with most of the land, and build a low-rise shopping center on the other part.

"The Native groups didn't feel like being told what to do: their plan was to leverage their legal status to build modern high rises, kinda like the Vancouver waterfront but bigger. It was an opportunity for them to succeed, ironically, because they weren't legally subject to the construction hurdles that crushed development in the city. The tribes had a kind of sovereign status. Well, these commissioners didn't want any Indians getting rich building the housing Portland needed. They wanted a goddamn wigwam museum thingie made outta fake wood, so they threatened to block the whole deal."

"Is that really what goes on around here?" Jesse asked, incredulous. "Kinda funny but also super fucked up."

"It gets better. Well, worse. And here's where Oscar comes in. The commissioners eventually agreed to let it go forward in exchange for a massive kickback. Of course they couldn't say any of this publicly. So 'Oscar' makes an appearance. Oscar was an acronym, another made up department with operatives under the chiefs of staff for the three commissioners. Not always the same guys. Oscar negotiated with the tribes, but was so greedy that the project could never work. The real business was obscured, but documents do exist, in order to give the restrictions force of law. The project even got its own office at the county. There's a locked door labeled 'Salmon Run River Delta Development Office' on the fourth floor. I've never gotten inside but I've gotten a few records brought out. They were sloppy, and no one paid attention since the whole deal collapsed, but that's HQ for whatever they got up to. I bet you find everything you're looking for in there."

Jesse whistled theatrically. Our waitress turned and gave him a look. Then she burst out laughing and we couldn't help but laugh as well.

"That's a hell of a tale. You were never tempted to publish this and blow the whole thing open?" I asked.

"It was tempting, especially when I was angry," Abby said. "Which was a lot. But I'm in this for the long game. Having some leverage for the future and maintaining relationships was the route I needed to take. If I'd taken them down, they'd just have gotten replaced with a new set of crazies and I'd be out of a job ... if you can call freelance journalism a job."

"Thank you," I said. And I meant it. "Your name won't come up. I'm just trying to pull together some evidence that my friend's family here" – I put my arm around Jesse – "are little Willamette Valley fish being hassled by bigger

Portland fish, who are being shaken down by even bigger Multnomah fish. Forget I said that. I sound ridiculous."

Abby smiled. "I get the idea. Honestly, fuck those guys. And let's eat."

Ronnie had just delivered our sandwiches: a Reuben, a cheeseburger, and a club, each nestled in a mountain of tots.

While we ate, I texted Hannah and asked if there was any chance troublemakers named Oscar might be a focus of interest at the county. Then I texted Manny asking if everything was going OK with Tyler and Isabelle.

We ordered more beer. The food was shockingly good or we were desperately hungry. I paid and looked at my phone as we walked to the door. I had a response from Hannah and one from Manny.

They read, respectively, "Yes" and "No."

43

The phone said it was 4:44 p.m., which meant there was barely time to get into the county building before it locked up for the day.

I sent Jesse to The Multnomah to check on Isabelle and Tyler and gave him Manny's number for a sync on his way over.

Getting to the county building took about five minutes, which I spent gaming out my approach. Upon arrival, I hopped in the elevator and emerged on four, wearing the ubiquitous lanyard. It wasn't the correct lanyard but it bore a color scheme and slogan that would pass. The badge holder identified me as a technical support contractor – which I was, for a couple of friends and for the bar underneath my apartment.

I asked the first person I encountered about the Salmon Run River Delta office. She had never heard of it but she accessed the internal directory and pointed me toward the northeast corner of the building. Sure enough, at the end of a hall which dead-ended on a window, a door marked only SRRDD stood on my left. Up to this point, I had been expecting an electronic fob or card entry: they're almost impossible to pick, so typical exploits ranged from social engineering to outright theft. Instead, I was staring down an old-school metal lock. The fact that most county employees "worked" from home meant that my first and second fumbled attempts didn't have an audience. Third time, right?

The office, a closet-like space with an impossibly high ceiling, had a narrow window but neither chair nor desk. I let the door close behind me. There were two locked filing cabinets: easy to penetrate although slow to search. There was also a table with a desktop computer – running, but password protected.

I looked at my watch. 4:58.

There was no easy way to exfiltrate masses of paper files and, without a lawyer's knowledge of what was in the docs and a lot more time to skim them, no way to find anything meaningful in situ.

I decided to rely on a sampling technique informed by questionable statistics and even more questionable literary theory: I grabbed a large empty hanging folder and stuffed it with fistfuls of pages from the beginning, middle, and end of the file sequence. I then divided the sequence twice more at about the quartile points and grabbed from there.

My phone buzzed with a message from Hannah: "If you're doing what I think you're doing, get the hell out of there. The feds are storming in five."

I looked at the big old computer, impossible to carry out in the current circumstance. I yanked the cord to kill the power and opened the machine. Like most office computers, the case was equipped with a lock slot to prevent what I was about to do. Like most office computers, the slot contained no lock. I pulled power and bus cables off the hard drive and used my knife to unscrew the drive from its bracket. I hoped the drive wasn't encrypted. For now, I threw it in my jacket pocket, hefted my selection of files under my arm, and pivoted to the door.

Before I touched the handle, an alarm went off. My heart skipped a beat before I realized it wasn't an intrusion alarm – it was a fire alarm. I dashed out of the tiny office and made for the exit stairs. As it happened, the alarm would have provided decent cover – if there had been anyone in the building to see me. This late afternoon, there was not. I briskly hopped steps to ground level and smashed the emergency door release to the street. It was too easy.

I kept checking for a tail but saw none as I zigzagged northeast toward Salmon and Southeast Ninth, just to get some space between me and whatever was going on.

I checked my phone again.

"Did you pull the fire alarm?" Hannah had texted.

"No. Maybe your fed friends did it as part of their entry tactics," I suggested.

"Negative. They're just pulling up now. Alarms were already blaring and fire bureau was on scene."

I texted a shrug emoji.

"Hold up. Apparently, there's an actual fire. You didn't do any of this?"

"Really? I thought we were friends."

"OK, well, get the hell away from there – looks like shit is going down."

"I'm gonna come back if I get to see them frog-march a commissioner. It would make everything worth it."

"Looks like they hoped to get their hands on the Oscar crew – some high-level staffers – but the intel was bad. They're in the wind."

I sent a thumbs-up tapback and started toward the river and downtown. I had a crazy guess where Oscar might be headed, but I needed to track Jesse, Tyler and Isabelle before I could indulge in my own goose chase.

Once I was in a rideshare headed across the river, I made a call to the marina.

"Hey, do I need an unlock to get to the *Anchor Tenant*? I got a case of champagne and twenty pounds of seafood on ice here and I'm already late with the delivery."

"I'm sorry to say it, but the *Anchor Tenant* just cast off."

"Ah, shit. This is gonna be my ass. Not to mention it's a couple thousand bucks of food. Are you sure they're gone? Maybe I can meet them. Which way did they sail?"

"They were sailing south, sir. I'm sorry about the timing. Must be a big party, though. Already took on a delivery including a ton of fresh stuff on ice."

"Yeah I guess it's pretty big. Thanks anyway. Any chance you could call me if they come back?"

"If they buy fuel or take anything on, I can do it. Otherwise we might not know."

"Thanks." I hung up. I expected the craft would be hosting quite an event and hoped to expand the affair by at least one. And, if the boat didn't come back north, then they couldn't be too far. Ever since the locks shut down at Willamette Falls, you couldn't sail south past Oregon City.

44

We were pulling up at The Multnomah and I jumped out to find Jesse walking in circles in the lobby.

"Hey Jack," he began.

"What happened?" I asked.

"By the time I got here, everyone was gone. I called Manny, like you said. Manny said he was keeping an eye on 'em. OK, he said he was kinda spying on them from the booth behind in the bar when they went to eat. Sounds like Tyler knew where Commissioner Perescelli's kids would be after school and said he had to go settle things about his mom. When he headed to the room to get his stuff, Manny walked up to Isabelle and explained his concerns, told her he was gonna follow Tyler and try to keep him out of trouble. At the time I talked with him, Manny was tailing Tyler down 43 toward Lake Oswego."

That would figure: the commissioner lived in Dunthorpe and had caught flack for sending her kids to private school in Lake Oswego instead of the perfectly respectable Riverdale public schools.

"Wait. Tailing? What was Tyler driving?" I asked.

Jesse looked glum. "He took my bike."

"And Isabelle?"

"Gone. Not here, not answering texts."

I thought for a minute. "Your car's still here, right? Let's go for a ride."

We got Jesse's car, swung by my apartment for a minute so I could grab some gear, and headed south.

While I drove, Jesse managed to get Tyler on the phone and tried to talk him down. From what I overheard, a lot of promises were made about futures Jesse couldn't guarantee. Worse, they were futures from a world Tyler didn't – and maybe wouldn't want to – inhabit. Negotiations seemed to be breaking down.

Mostly, I had to focus on my own phone call, to a dentist and Lake Oswego city councilor whose bacon I'd saved from a nasty frame-up. I was phoning the councilor to call in a favor: he had a dock on the river and a few small but beautiful fast boats.

Jesse's call ended before mine. When I got off the line, I looked over. "How'd it go?" I already knew the answer.

"Not great. Hung up on me. Said he didn't trust me, he had to take care of this himself, and he didn't want any part of working in the city. He'd rather live and die in the forest eating squirrel if he had to. Even the sports bar idea just seemed to enrage him."

"You did a lot of fast talking," I pointed out. "Didn't get real far."

"That's what I said!" he shot back.

"Try him again. If he picked up once he might another time. This time do more listening."

"Just keep him distracted?"

"Well, that's not the worst thing. But if it comes to it, tell him: leave the kids alone, he can come with us and we're going to get Perescelli."

"Is that true?"

"Sort of. It's more true than the tall tales you were spinning. Exigent circumstances."

"Huh?"

"Get on the horn, son. Tyler isn't thinking straight. You got about six minutes to convince him. I know where his head is at and that he wasn't dealt a full hand to begin with. But the cops – and Manny – will do what they need to do to protect those kids. Could go bad."

"Well, fuck," is all Jesse said in response before dialing the phone.

A few minutes later, I turned off of Riverside onto Briarwood. Here was access to magnificent riverfront homes which represented the lower Willamette's closest approximation to Tiburon or Malibu, albeit an Oregon experience at Oregon prices.

Momentarily, I pulled up in front of my old client's home, a modernist glass mansion done tastefully and accompanied by a suite of small outbuildings.

I hopped out of the car and I looked at Jesse expectantly.

"He's coming. I just have to text the address."

I unmoored the fastest and second-nicest of Dr. Leesworth's small collection of watercraft, grabbed the key which was visible where the doc told me he had "hidden" it, and waved Jesse to jump in. As he hopped the gunwale, the loud tearing of a dirt bike motor broke the stillness. Tyler hove into view on Jesse's bike and skidded straight across the lawn and onto the dock. We waved to Tyler and he leaped in. There would be time to apologize for the lawn damage later.

The river was now in shadow and carried a cold, pungent breeze. The boat gurgled, growled, and roared as I steered the craft toward the center of the channel where the water was deeper and the noise would attract less attention. Out of the corner of my eye, I saw Tyler's outstretched arm and, following the line to his fingertip, the thing which had seized his attention: on the dock, Manny was hollering inaudibly in our direction. A moment later, he hopped into one of the doc's slower ships, a small fishing boat. He looked around, sizing up his options, when a vehicle pulled to the end of the driveway. I wasn't one hundred percent sure from this distance, but I thought I saw Isabelle's graceful silhouette emerge.

"Jesse, see what's up with those two if you can," I said, turning my attention back to the river. At high summer, the river would have been an obstacle course of tiny craft: kayakers, canoers, stand-up paddle boarders, dragon boaters, along with sportsmen and drunk partiers. On this cold autumn evening, I mostly just needed to avoid logs and other debris that could do damage when I opened up the throttle.

In no time, we were bouncing around, transitioning and then on plane at almost thirty knots. The wind and spray along with the gathering darkness required my complete attention to piloting. We'd be at Willamette Falls in under ten minutes at this pace and I hoped to spy the *Anchor Tenant* before then. Several times, I saw something troubling – debris, an otter, a tiny abandoned boat – at the edge of my vision and had to cut the throttle lest we collide. I was sailing blind and eventually was forced to relent on the speed.

Checking my six, I saw Jesse and Tyler half embracing – I couldn't tell if they were praying or having a heart-to-heart. Beyond them I observed a distant light on the water and wondered if Manny or even Isabelle was following us southward.

As we rounded Goat Island and drew toward the Abernathy Bridge, I saw a yacht large enough to be the *Anchor Tenant*. I cut the throttle and dug out my binoculars. They confirmed Marrenhous' yacht, so I added just enough juice to make gentle upstream progress. All the lights were on and no one was visible on deck.

I explained my plan to Jesse and Tyler and they got ready with their phones. After passing a night vision camera to Jesse, I gently pulled astern the yacht, lucky not to damage either craft.

I hopped onto the transom ladder and pulled myself aboard, torn between getting down to business and keeping an eye on the young men behind me. Ultimately, they'd have to take care of themselves. With a final glance back, I headed forward.

The *Anchor Tenant*'s main deck was clear, so I prepared to climb down into the cabin. The lounge area I had spied on during my earlier voyage was illuminated but empty. I descended a steep ladder toward empty couches, the TV, and a massive spread of oysters, shrimp, crab, paté, caviar and ice buckets wrapping bottles of bubbly.

A further narrow staircase descended to a room deeper in the ship – I guessed sleeping quarters. The hatch was closed but light escaped from its rectangular edge. I approached and pressed my ear to the wood.

I heard heated voices. Drawing my gun and testing the unlocked door handle, I told myself things would not get any easier if I waited. I swung the hatch open. I believed my mind was open and prepared, that I couldn't be surprised.

In fact, I was surprised.

45

On my right, at the far end of the room, stood Chuck Marrenhous and his son Mark in cloyingly similar sea foam cotton dress shirts and gabardine trousers. They were flanked by the usual goons, all in black, one of whom held a FN Five-seveN pistol extended in front of him. None of this was the surprise.

In the center of the cabin was a bed and, on the other side, three men, also in matching outfits: plain white shirts and khaki chinos that made them look like airport missionaries.

These men were, presumably, Oscar, and that also did not surprise.

One of them held his hand to his abdomen where blood was soaking his shirt. My surprise came when the goon with the 5.7mm looked at me, shrugged, turned back to the bleeding man and, casually, fired another five or six rounds. The noise was deafening. In the low light of the cabin, the weapon sprayed a visible fireball about a foot in front of the muzzle.

I kept my hands where the goon could see them and I let the SIG dangle: I wasn't ready to bet my reflexes and my twelve rounds against the training and the fifteen-plus he might have ready to counter. I had to find words.

"We can end this here. You guys go home mostly happy," I said to the elder Marrenhous, "and these assholes," I gestured to the missionaries, "get federal prison. It's not a bad deal."

"I know who you are, Jack, and I know that you're not in a position to negotiate anything or to broker a deal here," Mark said. "Maybe you should get off of my boat before you end up like this clown," he continued, looking over at the corpse on the floor. Blood still dripped out of the man who'd stuck his arms into the cogs of power to extract a ransom and lost not just a promising career but his life.

"I'm glad you know who I am. It makes things easier because I'm not asking for anything. Not really. I'm offering a way out: asking, er, suggesting, that you forget everything you might have worked out with the county and – more importantly – everything you imagined working out with George Delany and his family's company. Get me the passwords, tell me where the computers and files are, I'll make them disappear."

"Why? How about, instead, you get off the boat before we fill you with holes and float your ass down to Astoria?"

"'Cause the feds are already coming. You can't make it downriver. And they don't want you. They want these wannabe Boss Tweeds in the business casual over here. That said, if they find him dead on the floor and your guys with the guns, it'd be pretty unlikely you walk."

"The files are all on the boat. We have to dump them into the river."

"There's no time for that – you need to leave."

"But you said they're coming upriver behind us."

"I've got a much faster boat tied astern. Take it, head downriver, and if you're lucky you'll blow right by them.

Consider this a learning experience. I know it hurts the ego to imagine, but these guys," I said, indicating the khaki-clad fools, "are bigger crooks than you. Instead of having a pissing contest, try some judo and let them take the fall. What was that you said the other day about your grandkids, Chuck?"

"Fuck it. Let's go," the elder Marrenhous muttered. Turning to me, he said, "I was just shooting off my mouth. Not sure I'm happy to be right. But, yeah, thanks to these shitheads, my grandkids won't get the twenty-first-century money I worked to get 'em. Instead, they'll get bits of a nineteenth-century world that money can't buy. Could be worse."

Chuck followed his men out the hatch and turned back to me. I showed my palms and shrugged. He gave a half salute.

I got a proper grip on my gun, dug up two sets of zip cuffs from my backpack and set about securing the living members of Oscar. I hoped that Jesse and Tyler had followed my instructions to video everything they could while staying out of sight.

As I knelt, tying up my prisoners, I heard twin outboards on Dr. Leesworth's boat spin up and then, a fraction of a second later, the hatch slam open. In the doorway stood another man in the missionary garb. Apparently, each of the commissioners had a man in Oscar. I started to wonder if the chair was directly involved, too, but the shiny automatic in the man's hand distracted me. Particularly when it started firing. It made less noise than the FN. More importantly, its handler was less competent. He missed with five rounds from under ten feet away, then rushed me. I leapt up and delivered a jumping kick before he could close the distance.

The firearm fell to the deck, but the man stumbled back, drew a miniature commando-style knife, and leaped onto the bed. I kicked again and he jumped, his arm swinging around and slashing my side. We wrestled as he tried to slash me again and fought to reach his gun. I struggled to immobilize his knife arm. He reached for the gun with his foot and I kicked air trying to push it away. I lost my grip on his hand and he drew back with the knife, while his knee pinned my arm. My free hand swung wildly.

An explosion reverberated through the cabin. And again. The man fell to my side and rolled off toward the wall. There was another explosion. I saw Tyler standing in the hatchway with his .357. He looked confused. He leaned against the bulkhead. Blood streamed out of his mouth and he swooned. A clang of metal rang out. The man I fought had grasped and raised his gun then dropped it on the deck as he died. But in between those events, he'd shot Tyler, who was slumped on the edge of the hatchway coughing gouts of blood. I got to him just as Jesse arrived from the outside. Tyler's eyes were almost blank. Jesse looked at me with eyes nearly as dead as his friend's. The boat shook violently and made a thunderous tearing, cracking sound.

I struggled to the cabin door.

"Someone better get the wheel," Jesse said, in a remote monotone.

"Huh?" I asked.

"The captain saw us when we came down here. Tyler pistol whipped him. There's no one at the helm."

I raced to the bridge. True enough, it was empty. Gas vapor lights from the old mill and other structures around Willamette Falls were right in my face – we were practically under the falls. I reached for the throttles but, before I could move them, the boat hit part of the old locks and spillway – a wall of submerged concrete and steel – and I was thrown violently to the port side.

The engines were still running and they were rotating the vessel in the turbulence of the falls. I got to my knees in time for the boat to hit something else and pitch up, causing me to slide out of the bridge entrance. I grabbed the ladder as I fell.

The yacht rolled to starboard. I wondered if it would capsize when I realized that was irrelevant: the hull had been breached. The lower deck was disappearing into the cold water.

I let go of the ladder and fell to the main deck. I looked down into the lounge, now dark and starting to fill with river.

"Jesse!" I screamed.

Where was he?

I leaned into the lounge and pointed a flashlight toward the hatch to the sleeping quarters. My beam illuminated Jesse holding Tyler below the armpits, trying to pull him up in the waist-deep, swirling water. It was never going to happen.

"Jesse, give me your hand!" I called, reaching down. "We have to go!"

"Where? Where are we gonna go?" he yelled back.

The boat shifted again, the water rose and Tyler slipped out of Jesse's grasp.

"Come on!" I yelled.

He took my hand. I pulled him as far as the main deck. Carried into the spray of the falls, the ship was listing and sinking. There were floatation rings around the rail. It was not obvious they'd be much help.

An airhorn pierced the roar. I looked downriver and a spotlight blinded me.

I squinted, wondering who it was. I had bluffed about the feds. They wouldn't be here anytime soon. The spotlight went out and I pointed the deck lantern into darkness.

Manny Gil, barely visible in all black, stood at the helm of a small boat about thirty feet away.

I tossed a floatation ring to Jesse and pointed to the port rail. He took it and jumped. I went after him. Once I oriented myself in the icy water, I tried to move downstream. I was paralyzed, bouncing and floating. I went under the roaring turbulence despite the PFD. I remembered a song I'd heard once, about getting a mouthful of water before you die and then another about a bright sunshine-filled day. I came up and immediately felt myself getting pulled under again. I couldn't resist it. I sank.

Then I rose and bashed painfully against metal. Something bright flashed behind me and I heard a crack.

Manny had dragged me against the hull of his craft using a boat hook. He reached for me, dropped the hook, and grasped my hands with his. Struggling despite the pain in my side, I got over the gunwale and flopped inside. Jesse was climbing on at the stern with a bit of help from Isabelle, whose face hovered in the night above an all-black tracksuit.

I looked at Jesse, Isabelle, and Manny and then passed out.

46

When I awoke, it felt like ages had elapsed. It was bright. Something smelled like Laphroaig. My side hurt. Where did I put that glass?

I turned to look for my drink and saw a patient monitor. My heart sank. There was no whiskey.

Outside the window was blue sky. A door swung open and a white coat entered followed by Jesse and Isabelle.

"How are you doing?" the doctor asked.

"I... I'm OK," I said. I looked down at my side and saw a massive bandage stained with bloody effluent. "A hospital? Did he really get me that bad?" I knew I had been cut but I was pretty sure it wasn't bad enough for an overnight stay.

"It's an ugly gash, lots of blood and it'll leave a hell of a scar. But no, that's nothing life threatening. Do you know why you're here?"

"Got me, doc."

"Your friends said you got hit in the back of the head in a boating accident. Definitely a concussion. Did some scans. You can probably go home this afternoon, you just have to follow the protocol." He motioned to Jesse and Isabelle and toward chairs in the room. They sat down. He shined an ophthalmoscope in my eyes and moved it around.

"Any questions?" the doc asked.

"Where am I? I mean, what hospital?"

"Hillsboro Community. Portland was pretty crazy last night and your friends were wise to bring you here instead." He looked at his smart watch then at his phone, tapped a few buttons on my EMR. "We'll try and get you home today," he said and walked out of the room.

Suddenly, I remembered. "Tyler. Oh my god. I'm so sorry."

Jesse's face was bandaged in two places, bruised purple in a couple more, and ashen elsewhere. His cheeks were sunken; eyes dark and focused a million miles away.

Isabelle took his hand as he choked back tears. "It's fucked up," he murmured. "All of it." He slumped in the chair.

Isabelle spoke up softly. "According to *The Oregonian*, a group of senior staff of the Multnomah County Commission was on a retreat last night when their boat was involved in a tragic accident."

I took a deep breath and sighed. Of course the world kept turning and the players kept spinning.

Isabelle read from her phone. "The Clackamas County Sheriff's Office Marine Unit is on the river recovering remains and collecting additional evidence. It is unclear why the yacht, which was piloted by an experienced captain and which enjoyed good sailing conditions, took on water, suffered an explosion, and ultimately sank in Willamette Falls last night."

I lifted myself painfully to a sitting position.

"Up for a walk?" Isabelle asked.

"If they're not gonna give me a drink, then I guess it's on me to get back in the game," I replied. I struggled to pull myself erect, smoothed my hospital gown, and looked for slippers or shoes. "Where did you have in mind?"

Isabelle smiled, put slippers where I could step into them, and handed me a cane. I looked like an idiot but I could walk just fine. She made a come-hither gesture and I followed her out the door. Jesse, shuffling, brought up the rear.

We went to the elevator, up one floor, and down a hall. Isabelle knocked then opened a door. I followed her in.

"*¡Bendito sea Dios!*" cried Altagracia Nuñez as I came through the doorway. "You saved my boy! Nothing will ever be enough thanks!" Behind her, in a hospital bed, was Fernando with a wide smile.

"*¡Qué bendición! Mi amigo, gracias mi amigo,*" said Fernando. "I'm pretty sure those guys were going to kill me."

"How is the shoulder?" I asked.

"This?" he pointed to the bandaged area. "Two surgeries. I'll be able to use it but I don't think I'll be able to pitch with it again."

On top of everything else, Fernando losing his pro ball dream hit hard. I joined Jesse, starting at the floor. "Man, I am so sorry," was all I could muster. I felt hollow inside. Somewhere, there was anger. And in between the anger and my mind was a gulf of pain.

"It's not that bad," Altagracia said.

"Yes, I understand. We have Fernando. That's the most important thing."

"No, I mean he has the other arm."

I looked up, my confusion visible.

"*Mi tío fue quien me enseñó a usar los dos brazos.*"

I was perplexed. My Spanish was not what it should be.

"My, uh…" Fernando started to translate.

"Uncle," interjected Isabelle.

"*Sí*, my uncle taught me baseball. I can pitch with both arms. Like Jurrangelo Cijntje and Pat Venditte! I'm not as good with the other arm – I'll have to work extra hard before next season. And I think the team is moving too."

A wave of happiness and relief flooded through me.

"You can switch pitch? That's a thing? Holy shit. That's the best news I've heard all week. I'm sure you'll be great!"

I turned to Jesse. "Thinking of opening a sports bar wherever the league moves the Pioneers off to?"

"I dunno," he replied. "Might see what I can get up to in Portland."

I couldn't resist taking a dig. "Portland, the cesspool ruining Oregon? Really?"

"No better or worse than home, I guess. Same wild west. Different characters, different stories, bigger buildings. No one's coming to help. Might as well saddle up."

About the author

Adam Breindel is a lifelong fan of mystery and detective stories. He lived in several American cities before moving to Portland and has discovered Oregon to be a uniquely compelling location for modern crime fiction. Adam studied math at the University of Chicago and classics at U Penn and at Brown. He works in the tech industry but did not allow AI to contribute any text to this book. Adam introduced detective Jack Louis in his first novel, *Bridgetown's Children*.

Made in the USA
Coppell, TX
22 January 2026

68924611R10142